The Wrong Arm of the Law

The two heavies neared our posh restaurant table. I tensed as one reached into a pocket, then relaxed as he pulled out an ornate golden badge.

"James diGriz? I am Captain Kretin of the planetary police. It is my duty—"

Police! Criminals might have given me some trouble, but I could polish off a squad of cops before breakfast and still have an appetite for lunch.

I leapt onto the long banquet table, neatly avoiding all the fine crockery with a precision that belies my years. When I reached the end, I spun about with my back to the window.

I was trapped. Every exit was blocked and the minions of the law were advancing.

"It's not that easy!" I shouted. "Better cops than you have tried to capture Slippery Jim diGriz!" I tensed my legs and sprang backwards, crashing through the window and hurtling out into the night.

"Thus ends the saga of the Stainless Steel Rat!"

Don't bet on it! The fun's just beginning in
The Stainless Steel Rat for President

The Stainless Steel Rat
for President

Harry Harrison

BANTAM BOOKS
TORONTO • NEW YORK • LONDON • SYDNEY • AUCKLAND

THE STAINLESS STEEL RAT FOR PRESIDENT
A Bantam Spectra Book / December 1982
8 printings through July 1988

ISBN 0-553-27612-3

Published simultaneously in the United States and Canada

Bantam Books are published by Bantam Books, a division of Bantam Doubleday Dell Publishing Group, Inc. Its trademark, consisting of the words ''Bantam Books'' and the portrayal of a rooster, is Registered in U.S. Patent and Trademark Office and in other countries. Marca Registrada. Bantam Books, 666 Fifth Avenue, New York, New York 10103.

PRINTED IN THE UNITED STATES OF AMERICA

O   17   16   15   14   13   12   11   10   9   8

1

"Can you think of a special toast?" I asked, watching closely as the waiter filled our glasses with the sparkling vintage wine.

"I certainly can," my dear Angelina said, raising her glass and looking across it straight into my eyes. "To my husband, Jim diGriz, who has just saved the universe. Again."

I was touched. Particularly by the *again*. Since I am by nature extremely modest, it is always a pleasure to have my personal feelings about my abilities supported by an unsolicited testimonial. Particularly from one as lovely, charming, intelligent, and dangerously ruthless as my Angelina. She had also been present during the entire affair with the Slimeys, had even been an active participant while I was stopping them from taking over our galaxy, so I treasured her opinion even more.

"You are too kind," I murmured. "But truth will out. However it is all over now and we will forget the grim parts, drink to the victories—and enjoy the best meal that this restaurant can provide."

We touched glasses and drank deep. Over my wife's shoulder I admired the orange Blodgett sun setting behind the purple skyline, the sunlight striking reflections from the canal outside. And out of the corners of my eyes I kept close watch on the two heavies seated by the door who had our table under subtle surveillance. I didn't know who they were—but I did know that they were packing large guns in their damp armpits.

I would not let them spoil the occasion! Angelina and I made light talk, drank the wine, gorged ourselves on the curried mastodon. The string quartet played, darkness fell, we lingered over coffee and liqueur—and Angelina took out a tiny mirror as she touched up her lipstick.

1

"You do know that there are two thugs by the entrance who have been watching us closely ever since we arrived."

I sighed and nodded and took out my cigar case. "Unhappily, my sweet, I do. I did not mention them for fear they would spoil the meal."

"Nonsense! It just added a little spice to the dinner."

"Most perfect wife," I enthused, smiling as I lit my cigar. "This planet radiates boredom. Anything with the slightest whiff of interest can only be an improvement."

"I'm glad you feel like that . . ." She glanced into her mirror. "Because they are on their way over here now. Is there anything I can do to help? I only have this tiny evening bag, so I'm not really prepared. Just a few grenades, a sonic bomb or two, nothing important."

"Is that all?" I asked, eyebrows reaching for my hairline. My Angelina never ceases to amaze.

"No. This lipstick is a one-shot pistol, deadly at fifty meters . . ."

"We won't need that," I said hurriedly. "Not for just two of them. You sit and watch. A little exercise to aid my digestion."

"Four. They've been joined by some friends."

"The odds are still in my favor."

I could hear them thudding up behind me now—and I relaxed. From the weight of their steps they could only be police. Criminals might have given me some trouble. But the local police! I could polish off a squad before breakfast—and still have an appetite for lunch. The footsteps stopped as the burliest one appeared before me. I tensed as he reached into a pocket—then relaxed as he produced nothing more deadly than an ornate golden badge studded with precious stones.

"I am Captain Kretin of the Blodgett police. While you, I believe, are the individual who operates under the alias of the Stainless Steel Rat . . ."

Alias indeed! As though I were a common criminal. I ground my teeth with rage as I reached out and broke my cigar under his nose. His eyes widened—then closed, as the instant sleeping gas from the crunched vial in the cigar drifted into his hairy nostrils. I took his badge, after all he had offered it to me, and turned aside as he dropped, face first, into the sugar bowl.

I kept turning, my rigid index finger extended, to catch his corpulent colleague just behind the jawbone with this deadly digit. There is a nerve ganglion there which, if hit in the precise center, will produce instant unconsciousness. I did not miss. He folded nicely across his fat friend.

I didn't stay around to watch. "Twenty-two," I called out to Angelina as I started for the kitchen door. Before I reached it two more policemen stepped through. And the main entrance was blocked by survivors of the original four.

"Trapped!" I shouted aloud, then touched the sonic screamer in my belt buckle. A number of the diners screamed in response as the vibrations produced feelings of terror. Nice. In the confusion I would escape through the fire exit hidden behind the drapes.

Except this door wasn't the only thing the drapes concealed. Two more policemen blocked my way. This was getting annoying. I leapt onto a long banquet table and neatly danced my way down its length, avoiding all the crockery with a fine precision that belies my years. More screams and shouts followed this exhibition until I reached the end—and spun about with my back to the window.

I was trapped. Every exit was blocked, and the minions of the law were advancing.

"It's not that easy!" I shouted. "Better cops than you have tried to capture Slippery Jim diGriz! All have failed. Better a clean death than sordid captivity!"

Behind the attacking hordes I could see my sweet Angelina blowing me a farewell kiss. I gave her a last wave as I tensed my legs and sprang backwards.

"Thus ends the saga of the Stainless Steel Rat!"

My words were followed instantly by the crash of breaking glass, as I burst through the window and hurtled out into the night.

Falling. Twisting and turning as I did. So that I hit the waters of the canal in a clean dive that took me under in a curving arc. I did not break the surface again until I was some meters away and concealed by the darkness.

It was a happy end to a pleasant evening; I hummed to myself as I did an easy breaststroke through the darkness. I had brought joy to this dull planet, at least for a few brief moments. The police had reluctantly indulged in a bit of exercise. Now they could relax and fill out the endless reports so dear to the copper's heart. The news reporters would have something interesting to write about—for a change—and the populace in turn would be fascinated by the exciting events of the evening. I really should be treated as a benefactor of mankind—not a criminal. But there is no justice, I knew that, so I just swam on.

Number twenty-two was a safe house located in one of the more repellent districts of Blodgett City. Angelina would know what the number meant and would join me there. Meanwhile, there was little chance that my sodden clothing would draw the attention of anyone foolish enough to be abroad in these mean streets. There was one hidden entrance to the house that began in a public toilet, which I used now as being the most appropriate. In the house I left a trail of ruined clothing down the hallway to the bath, where a steaming shower relaxed and restored me. I was dressed again in fresh garments and sipping a reviving drink when Angelina let herself in by a more acceptable doorway.

"A remarkable exit," she said.

"I hoped you would enjoy it." I pointed. "You have left the door open by mistake, my sweet."

"No mistake, my love," she answered. As an attacking herd of policemen thundered through behind her.

"Betrayed!" I shrieked, leaping to my feet. "*Et tu, Brute?*"

"I'll explain," she said, coming towards me.

"Mere words will not explain treachery!" I shouted as I dived around her towards the escape panel in the wall. She extended a delicate foot that caught my ankle and sent me sprawling headlong. Before I could rise again the hordes of policemen had fallen upon me.

2

I'm good—but not that good. Sheer weight of numbers overwhelmed me. The first two attackers dropped unconscious, as did the next two. But someone had a armlock on me and as I was breaking this hold another policeman got me by the ankle. And so on. Roaring with rage, like a giant pulled down by ants, I fell beneath the onslaught. My last act was to free my right arm long enough to take the jeweled policeman's badge from my pocket and flip it across the room to land at Angelina's feet.

"Here!" I ululated. "You deserve that. Not as a souvenir as I had planned, but as a decoration honoring your new and traitorous alliance with the police!"

"How charming," she said, picking it up, then stepping forward and swinging a sharp uppercut that caught me square on the jaw. "And that is *your* decoration for mistrusting your wife. Release the creature."

I dropped, stunned, as the restraining hands let go. Angelina throws a mean punch. When the whirling constellations had vanished, and vision returned, I saw her handing the badge back to the policeman at her side.

"This is Captain Kretin," she said, "who tried to speak to you earlier this evening. Are you ready to listen now?"

I muttered something that even I couldn't understand and stumbled to the nearest chair, rubbing my jaw and feeling immensely sorry for myself. The captain spoke.

"As I have been explaining to your charming wife, Mr. diGriz, we merely want you to aid in an investigation. A man has been found, brutally murdered . . ."

"I didn't do it! I was out of town at the time! I want my lawyer . . ."

"Jim, *darling*, listen to the nice policeman."

It was the way she said *darling* that sent ice water through

5

my veins. I shut up. My Angelina can be deadly when provoked.

"You misunderstand; no one is accusing you of the crime. We just need your aid in attempting to solve this hideous felony. This is the first murder we have had on Blodgett in a hundred and thirteen years, so we are kind of out of practice with this sort of thing."

The captain took out his notebook to refresh his memory, then carried on in a boring and monotonous voice. "Earlier this afternoon, at approximately thirteen hundred hours, there was a disturbance in the Zaytoun district of this city, not far from your place of residence. Witnesses reported three men running from the scene of the crime. The police were summoned and found the victim of the assault, who had been brutally stabbed a number of times. He died without regaining consciousness. His pockets were empty, his wallet missing, he had no identification of any kind on his person. However, during the subsequent post mortem examination a piece of paper was found in his mouth. This is the piece of paper." He held out a wrinkled scrap, and I took it up gingerly.

Scrawled on it were the words STAINLUS STEAL RATA.

"Whoever wrote this doesn't spell too well," I muttered, brain still addled from Angelina's tiny but deadly fist.

"A remarkable observation," she said, looking over my shoulder. Her tone of voice was not a sympathetic one. The policeman droned on.

"It is our theory that the victim was attempting to contact you. If this is so, then the indications are that he put the paper into his mouth when he was attacked, in order to conceal its presence from his assailants. Here is his picture. We would like to ascertain the dead man's identity."

He passed it over. I blinked my eyes into focus and stared at it. I was depressed. I have seen corpses before so that part didn't bother. It was a good holograph, in three-dimensional color, clear and sharp. I turned it around and around—then handed it back.

"That's all very interesting," I said. "But in all truth I have never seen this man before."

They didn't want to believe me, but in the end they had no choice. I could see that they were sure that I was lying—even though I was telling them the absolute truth. They left after some more futile questions, carrying away three of their party who had not regained consciousness. I went to the bar to mix us some strong drinks, since it had turned out to be a very trying evening. But when I turned about with the glasses in my hands I found the point of a very sharp kitchen knife about one centimeter from my left eyeball.

"Now what was that you said about my being a traitor?" Angelina asked in a warm, cold voice; honey over ice.

"My love!" I gasped, stepping backwards. The knife moved with me, never changing its relative position. I felt the sweat break out on the nape of my neck as I began lying swiftly. "How could you be so heartless? So misunderstanding? When the police appeared I was sure they had captured you, forced you to lead them here against your will. So I called you a traitor so they would think you were not involved in whatever charge they were arresting me on. I did it but to protect you my dearest!"

"Oh, Jim, I have been so cruel to you!" The knife clattered to the floor and she had her arms about me and I juggled fiercely not to spill the drinks down her back. Her arms were strong, her embrace warm, her kisses passionate. And I felt like a rat.

"There, there," I gasped after we came up for air. "Just a misunderstanding. Now let us drink our drinks and try to figure out just what the hell is going on around here."

"Were you really telling them the truth? You've never seen the dead man before?"

"The truth and nothing but! I know that I have broken my long-standing rule of never telling the police anything that might aid them in the slightest. It can't hurt, just this once. The man's an absolute stranger."

"Then let us find out who he is." She took the holograph from behind the seat of the sofa where she had concealed it. "I took this from the captain's pocket as he left. There is no need to involve the local police in Special Corps matters. I'll get on to the local agent at once."

She was right of course. This affair undoubtedly had ramifications that stretched far beyond this backward planet. Since identity records here were exhaustively complete it meant that the dead man had to be from off-planet. Which meant that the case now was the responsibility of the legendary, galaxy-wide, professional, superior and all-embracing police force known only as the Special Corps. Of which organization I can say, in all modesty, I am the most important member.

"We'll need more identification than this picture," I said, handing it back to her. "Have the agent meet us here. I'll be back within the hour with everything that he will need for the investigation."

I slipped a tool kit into my pocket before leaving. The city morgue was not too distant—which will give you a good idea of the kind of neighborhood this is—and I went through a back window and three locked doors without slowing down. I pick locks the way others pick their teeth.

I slid out the drawer of the cooler and stared down at the corpse. The glimmering hope that he might be familiar in the frozen flesh vanished. The mystery remained. It took but seconds to scrape off fragments of skin, clip hair samples—and extract dirt from under the man's nails. His clothes had been carefully filed and labeled by the police. I located them and took samples of these as well. And still more scrapings from his shoes. After this I went out the way that I had gotten in—and no one knew of either my arrival or departure. This minor operation had gone so smoothly that I returned to the safe house just as the Special Corps agent was letting himself in through the public convenience.

"Nice weather today, Mr. diGriz," he said, adjusting his clothing.

"It's always nice on Blodgett, Charley. That's why I hate it. When is the next shipment going out to headquarters?"

"A couple of hours. The weekly bag. I'm taking it myself."

"Perfect. I want you to take along these containers. Tell the lab to use every possible test on these samples. Here's a picture of the late deceased that I took them from. Get me gene tests, pollen tests, blood groups, ethnotyping, everything and anything they can think of. I want to know who this man is—or was. If he can't be identified I want to know where he came from. He was looking for me—and I'm very interested in finding out why."

The answer came in a surprisingly short time. Just three days later the front door bell rang and I looked into the scanner to see that the good and faithful Charley had returned. I let him in and reached out for the sealed case he was carrying. He pulled it away and chewed nervously at his lower lip. I growled deep in my throat and he cringed even more.

"I got orders, Mr. diGriz. From Inskipp, the supremo, our Commander-in-Chief."

"And what does that dear, sweet man have to say for himself?"

"He says that you have forged some checks on the Corps secret account and he wants the seventy-five thousand credits back before he releases any more information to a depraved crook . . ."

"You're calling me a depraved crook!"

He whinnied with fear as he scurried away from my grasping fingers.

"No! You got me wrong! I didn't say that—Inskipp did. I'm just quoting him like he told me to."

"The bearer of ill-tidings should be killed as well," I snarled, my fingers still snapping in anger. I reached for him again but Angelina appeared suddenly and stepped between us. She held out a check to Charley.

"Here is the money we *borrowed* from the account. A simple error in bookkeeping, wouldn't you say?"

"I sure would! I do the same thing myself sometimes." He wiped the sweat from his brow and passed over the case. "If you will kindly give this to your husband I'll be moving on. A busy day coming up, ha-ha." The door slammed behind his back and I took the case from Angelina, pretending that I did not see the angry flare of her nostrils.

"This is it," I said, pressing my thumb on the security latch. The case fell open, a screen lifted up and glowed with life. Inskipp's depressing features looked out at me and I almost dropped the thing. Angelina must have seen my expression because she took the case from my hands and placed it on the end table. The imaged Inskipp glowered and snarled and shook a piece of paper in my direction.

"You've got to stop stealing this organization's money, diGriz. It sets a bad example for the troops. You will have paid back your last embezzlement by now or you wouldn't be listening to this message. It's only because of our interest in Paraiso-Aqui that I am talking to you now."

"What is Paraiso-Aqui?" I said aloud.

The image nodded sagely. "By now you are asking yourself what is Paraiso-Aqui." The smugness and self-assurance of the man. How easy it is to hate your boss. Particularly when he is one jump ahead of you. "Well I'll tell you. It is the home world of the murdered man you asked the lab to track down. I want you to go there and have a look at this planet. Then come and report to me. If you will read the document enclosed here you will quickly see what our interest is."

The image vanished and the screen went dark. I flipped the screen back into its well and took up the envelope that had been concealed beneath it.

"This is very interesting," I said, quickly flipping through the printed sheets.

"In what way?"

"Because not only don't I know the man who was trying to see me—but I have never in my life heard of his home world before."

"Well . . . we are just going to have to do something about that, aren't we?"

"We certainly are!" I said, smiling in return. "We are just going to have to grit our teeth and obey Inskipp's instructions. Like it or not we will have to visit this mysterious planet." Angelina nodded and we just stood there grinning like fools. Knowing—without knowing how we knew—that the present period of peaceful boredom was at an end. The future was already looking brighter. I felt it in my bones. Something very unusual and highly interesting was about to begin.

3

The travel brochure was heavy and warm to the touch, the copy on its cover glowing with self-importance. "Come to sunny perfection on the holiday world of Paraiso-Aqui," I read aloud.

Angelina, sitting at my side, was reading from a more sober and thinner volume, appropriately bound in black.

"Paraiso-Aqui is a planet that was settled during the first galactic expansion and only recently rediscovered. It is noteworthy for having the most corrupt form of government in the galaxy."

"A slight difference of opinion between these two sources," I said, rubbing my hands together with anticipatory glee.

"Afternoon bouillon, sir?" the steward-robot asked, bowing and scraping before us.

"Not even to bathe in, you mechanized toady," I said. "I'll have a large Altairian panther juice on the rocks. Better make that two—"

"One," Angelina said firmly. "Bouillon for me."

"Yes, madam, delighted, perfect choice, wonderful," the obsequious machine salivated, bowing and nodding and rubbing its hands together as it writhed away. I hated it. Just as much as I hated everything else about this space-going cruise ship, the Luxurious Paradise Planet Tour, as well as all of the repulsive and loathsomely garbed tourists who gathered in shrieking throngs throughout the lounge.

"But we're dressed the same way, my darling," Angelina said. I must have spoken my thoughts aloud in the passion of the moment. And we were indeed dressed the same way. With a vengeance! I wore a short-sleeved shirt patterned with hideous purple and yellow blossoms. With shorts to match. Angelina wore exactly the same outfit, admittedly filling hers out in a far more attractive way. Also, in the latest holiday fashion, we had our hair dyed blonde and curled into

11

little green-tipped ringlets. I would have felt like an absolute
fool were it not for the fact that all of our fellow travelers
were garbed and coiffed in an equally repulsive fashion. A
perfect disguise, yes, but what a price it exacted from my free
soul! I opened the brochure to reveal a holopic of a deep blue
sea under a light blue sky. The waves stirred and crashed
onto the beach with a tiny crashing sound; a faint smell of sea
brine wafted up from the page.

"Happy natives laugh away their days in the sunshine
amidst the gustatory glories of sun-ripened fruit and fresh-
caught fish."

Angelina read quietly from her book, a dark counterpoint
to mine.

"The inhabitants live in a condition of near-slavery; poverty
and disease is the norm. The rule of the dictator's government is absolute."

"*Thirty minutes to planetfall . . . planetfall in thirty minutes,*" the loudspeakers whispered. The tourists stirred and
squeaked with excitement. I threw my guidebook into the
atomic oubliette where it exploded with a puff of smoke, thin
cries echoing from its recorded pages.

"We'll just have to see for ourselves," I said. Angelina
handed me the Special Corps report and I nodded and sent it
after the other. "If that is found in our luggage we are
finished before we even begin."

The steward smarmed up and we took our drinks. Angelina
smiled across her steaming cup at me. "Now, don't be a
spoilsport, Jim diGriz. This is not only a cover, but is a real
holiday as well. You're going to enjoy it if I have to throttle
you into submission. Think of it as a second honeymoon—
no, a *first* one! We never did have a proper one."

"Aren't we a little late? After all the twins are almost
twenty years old . . ."

"Which makes me hideous, middle-aged and unattractive I
suppose?" There was ice in her words and menace in her
voice. I threw my drink aside—it ate a hole in the carpet
where it fell—and dropped on my knees before her.

"Angelina mine! Light of my life! More beautiful with each
passing day!" Which was true enough; she was curved and
warm and lovely, with more of her delicate pink skin out of
the holiday outfit than in it. I seized her hands and kissed her
fingers passionately and all of the tourists cheered while she
smiled and nodded.

"That's more like it," she said. "A little holiday from crime will do us both a world of good."

Then we were on the ground and the lock was opened; warm air and sweet music rolled in from outside. I settled my camera around my neck, put on my sunglasses, took Angelina by the arm and joined the ecstatic throng. Their happiness was catching. Angelina caught it, smiling and laughing with the others, humming along with the catchy music. I was immune. I chortled and grimaced with the best of them, but inside it was the same old hot-tempered and cold-blooded diGriz who peeped out at the world.

But it was hard to be a curmudgeon in a place like this. The spaceport was sited at the ocean's edge; the salt tang in the air was delicious and sharp. The sun was as warm as advertised. Smiling native girls, bare-busted and buxom, greeting the tourists with wreaths of flowers and tiny bottles of some golden beverage. I pocketed the bottle and sniffed the flowers, pretending indifference to the mammalian magnificence on all sides, knowing full well that Angelina had her steely eyes on me. The crowd of voyagers moved forward so smoothly that within a few moments we were facing the official at passport control. He was as brown-skinned and smiling as the girls, but was wearing a shirt, no doubt to demonstrate his executive position.

"*Bonvenu al Paraiso-Aqui,*" he said, extending his hand. "*Viaj pasportoj, mi petas.*"

"So you speak Esperanto on this planet," I said, responding in the same language as I passed over my interstellar identity card. Forged of course.

"Not everyone," he said, still smiling, as he slipped the card into the machine before him. "Our language is the beautiful Español. But everyone you will meet will speak Esperanto, have no fear." He looked at the machine's screen while he talked, which of course revealed nothing except the blandest untrue information about me. When he returned the card he pointed to the gadget-covered camera about my neck.

"That is indeed a fine photographic apparatus you have there."

"It should be—cost me more credits than you see in a year I bet, ho-ho."

"Ho-ho," he echoed, the smile not quite so sincere now. "May I look at this machine?"

"Why? It's just a camera."

"There are certain regulations about cameras, you see."

"Why? Got something to hide?"

The smile was definitely pasted on now and his fingers were twitching. I smiled back—then passed over the camera. "Careful now, that's a delicate machine."

He took it from me and the back instantly sprang open. As it had been rigged to do. Coils of film rolled out. I grabbed it back.

"Now look what you've gone and done!" I wailed. "Spoiled all the film of my wife and our friends on the ship, and everything."

I struggled with the film and ignored his apologies—and walked past him with Angelina at my side. All according to plan. Our luggage was clean and we had no concealed devices about our persons. But the camera was a masterpiece of complicated gadgetry. It would take pictures—and do a number of other interesting things, all of which were strictly illegal. The day was starting well.

"My goodness, look at that!" Angelina squealed, an exact imitation of the other squeals rising on all sides.

"Are they dangerous?"

"What are they?"

"Please, ladies and gentlemen, if I could have your attention." A uniformed guide spoke to us through a voice amplifier. "My name is Jorge and I am your tourist representative. If you have any questions, please come to me. I will now answer the first question that I know you are all asking. These friendly creatures between the traces of the little wagons are known as *caballos* in our language. Their history is lost in the midst of time, but the story is told that they came with us from the legendary planet called Earth, or Dirt, the fabled home of mankind. They are our friends, harmless creatures who pull our wagons and till our fields. Unprotesting and happy, they will convey you to your hotels. We leave!"

The *caballos*, and their rickety wagons, combined to provide one of the most uncomfortable modes of transportation I had ever had the misfortune to experience. And they weren't *caballos* at all but hay-burning horses which I had encountered before during an unplanned trip through time to Earth, the very real and unlegendary home of all mankind. But I wasn't mentioning that in the present company. Who, despite the discomfort of the journey, were laughing and calling out shrilly to each other. Even Angelina seemed to be enjoying herself. I felt like a skeleton at a wedding.

"Whee," I said, attempting to get into the spirit of the thing. I dug into my pocket and extracted the bottle of amber liquid the welcoming girl had given me. Undoubtedly some loathsome native concoction made from rotted fruit or old socks. I uncapped it and drained it. "Whee!" I said, and meant it this time. I called to Jorge who had the nerve to actually straddle and ride one of the horses. He thundered over at my command. I held up the bottle for his examination.

"What is this stuff, pardner? Liquid sunshine? Best booze I have tasted since I was weaned."

"We are pleased that you like it. It is made from the fermented juice of the *caña* and is called *ron*."

"Well, baby, this ron stuff is something else again. Only thing wrong with it is that it comes in such small bottles."

"In all sizes," he laughed, and dug into his saddle bag to extract another bottle of more reasonable dimension.

"How can I ever thank you?" I enthused, snatching it from his grip.

"Easily. It will appear on your bill." He galloped away.

"Not going to get polluted this early in the day, are you?" Angelina asked as I lowered the bottle from my lips and sighed.

"Never, my sweet. Just getting in the old holiday mood. Join me?"

"Later. I'm enjoying the scenery now."

It was indeed something to see. Our road wandered in easy loops down through green fields to the shore. The sand glistened cleanly in the sun and the blue ocean beckoned. Very nice. But where were the locals? Other than the drivers and Jorge there were none of them in sight. We were getting the tourist treatment all right. Fine, Jim, enjoy it for the moment. Don't be a spoilsport.

"Why look there, papa," one of my fellow tourists called out in ringing tones. "Aren't they just too cute for words?"

I looked there and didn't think they were cute at all. If anything they looked kind of miserable despite the smiles directed our way. A group of men and women were working in the field beside the road. Cutting down the tall green plants with long and lethal-looking knives. The sun was hot, the work hard, and if they weren't fatigued and drenched with sweat they weren't human. I raised the camera and clicked off some shots.

Our driver turned about in his seat when he heard the buzz of the mechanism—so I photographed him as well. For a moment his fixed smile almost slipped, then his white teeth shone in a grin.

"You must save your film for the beautiful gardens and the beautiful hotel," he said.

"Why? Is there anything wrong with taking pictures of the people working in the fields?"

"No, of course not, but it is so uninteresting."

"Not to the people there. They looked tired. How many hours a day do they work?"

"I have no way of knowing those things."

"What do they get paid?"

I was talking to his back. He shook the reins and did not answer me. I caught Angelina's eye and winked. She nodded back.

"I think I'll try some of that ron now," she said.

The hotel was as luxurious as promised, our quarters expensively attractive. Our luggage was waiting—well-searched no doubt—and I left Angelina to do the unpacking. Since I was sure that all of my fellow tourists were male chauvinist pigs—unlike me—I was forced to fall into that role no matter how personally unattractive I found it.

"See you around when you finish that, honey," I said, then quickly slipped out the door before I could hear her forceful rejoinder.

I pottered about the grounds, looked in on the bar, then stopping awhile by the swimming pool. I started to take a photograph of a few of the attractively nude female sunbathers, then desisted when a chill passed through me at the thought of Angelina's reaction if she happened to run across this picture. Very possessive, my wife, and I loved it. I think. I wandered on and found the tourist shop.

It took an effort not to shudder at the little ships made of gilded clamshells, the cutesy sailor caps lettered with inspiring messages such as KISS ME YOU MAD, PASSIONATE FOOL! and KEEP ON CLANKING! With averted eyes I passed them and went on to a section filled with souvenir cards and guide books. I was looking them over when a soft voice spoke in my ear.

"May I help you, sir?"

Lovely, young, limpid eyes, full of figure, golden of skin, ruby-lipped and as exotic as a tiger . . .

"You certainly can!" I said hoarsely, then restrained my enthusiasm. Not with Angelina on the same planet! "I want . . . that is I want a guide book."

"We have many excellent ones. Anything in particular?"

"Yes. A history of Paraiso-Aqui. Not a propaganda puff for tourists, but something real. Do you have anything like that?"

She penetrated me with a low and smoky gaze—before turning to the shelves. When she turned back she had a thick volume in her hand that she extended to me.

"I think you will find what you want in here," she said before turning lithely and walking slowly away.

To work, Jim! I told myself, pulling my eyeballs away from her fascinating form and fixing them on the book before me.

A *Social and Economic History of Paraiso-Aqui*. Wonderful. Sounded like a best seller. I flipped through it and instantly found the piece of paper between its pages. There were block letters printed on it which I could read without removing it from its lair.

BEWARE! DO NOT BE SEEN WITH THIS!

A sudden shadow obscured the page; I closed the book and looked up. A heavyset local stood before me. Smiling insincerely.

"I would like that book," he said, extending his hand.

I could see the word as clearly as if he had it painted on his forehead. COP. That was the word. Policeman. A familiar breed around the galaxy.

"My goodness, what do you want my poor little book for?" I asked.

"That is not your concern. Give."

"No." I stepped back, trembling with mock fear. He smiled coldly at this and reached out to take the book from my cowardly hands.

My holiday was beginning at last!

4

I let him get both hands on the book before I reached out and grabbed his rather prominent nose and gave it a strong tweak. For no reason other than sadism, I am forced to admit. He roared with rage, revealing a mouth full of crooked teeth badly in need of dental attention. Then his mouth closed, as did his eyes, as he dropped heavily to the floor. A strong finger jabbed firmly into the nerve ganglion of the solar plexus will produce instant unconsciousness. I turned away from the scene of this minor triumph to find one of the locals, in hotel staff uniform, standing behind me. Eyes like saucers, mouth slightly agape.

"He must have been very tired to fall asleep like that," I said. "But this planet is so relaxing. I want to buy this book."

He blinked down at the cover and found his voice. "I am sorry, but that is not one of our books."

Now it was my turn to blink. "It must be. I saw the other clerk take it from the shelf."

"There is no other clerk. Just myself."

Realization penetrated. I shrugged and turned to leave. No clerk and no book. I had been set up, that was obvious. And as soon as sleeping beauty recovered the minions of the law would be howling on my tail. How nice of them to supply some diversions for me on this boring holiday world. Angelina was just slipping into a bathing suit when I returned, which instantly triggered my libido. After a brisk session of kissing and smooching she gently pushed me away.

"We must go on holiday more often if it will bring out the healthy beast in you like that. What is the book?"

"Nothing at all. I just picked it up. Let us go for a stroll on the beach so I can see if your swimsuit matches the sand." I produced a roll of the eyes as I said this. She nodded slightly, showing she understood.

"Wonderful. Let me find my sandals."

We exited in silence and it wasn't until we were walking at the water's edge, far from any of the buildings, that she spoke.

"Do you think the room is bugged?"

"Don't know. I just didn't want to chance it when I opened this book." I explained what had happened as I found the note and slipped it from between the pages. There were a few brief lines of writing inside it that we read in silence.

> *The people of this planet desperately need your help. Aid us, we beg. Please walk on the beach alone at 2400 this night.*

There was no signature. I bent and scooped up a handful of water and pulped the note in it, then kicked the shreds into the sand as I walked.

"I wonder who they are?" Angelina asked. I nodded solemn agreement to this.

"That is the important question, isn't it? I was obnoxious to the passport official, took photographs of the laboring peasantry—and asked nosy questions. My presence is known. I am contacted. But, as you so rightly ask—by whom? This note could be from the desperate citizens of Paraiso-Aqui, anxious that the galaxy be informed of their plight . . ."

"Or it could be a trap set by the security forces to get you into trouble."

"My thoughts exactly. But I have no choice. Behind the barn at midnight to meet my destiny. Though it may be difficult."

"Why?" she asked, squinting deliciously up at me in the actinic glare of the sun.

"Because that heavy is going to come looking for me when he recovers consciousness. We don't know who left the note—but I am certain of the policeman's identity."

"Then that takes care of your midnight appointment. When the police come for you, why then you just lead them a merry chase, something I know you always enjoy. And I will keep the appointment in your place."

"Dearest! The danger!"

She smiled warmly and squeezed my arm tenderly. "How sweet! You're worried about me."

"No, not in the slightest. Just concerned for the safety of this other lot if they try some funny business with you."

"Beast," she said, her gentle grip changing to an iron claw that bit deep into my bicep. Then she smiled. "But you're right, of course. Things have been quiet. I rather hope that whoever is coming does try on something funny."

"It's settled then." I rubbed at my bruised arm. "Let's get back to the room and order up some food. I don't want to do a lot of running around on an empty stomach."

The first thing we saw when we came into the room was the unconscious man stretched out on the floor beside the bed, his arms still reaching towards my camera which was resting innocently in the middle of the counterpane.

"That's number one," I said. "He let himself in to wait for us, then passed the time by trying to take a look at the camera. Automatic sleeping gas release got him."

"Police," Angelina said, going quickly through his pockets. "Identification, gun, blackjack, handcuffs, hunting knife and stun grenades. A very nasty type."

"Agreed. All is not paradise on Paraiso-Aqui. You had better keep the camera with you. I'll just slip a few items out of it to take with me. Now let us order the food before we have any more visitors."

Room service was fast and efficient. Within a few minutes the waiter arrived, wheeling in a trolley heavy-laden with succulent goodies. Unhappily two uniformed policemen wheeled in right behind him.

"Leave this room at once," Angelina said, stepping forward to block their way. "You have not been invited in." The waiter cringed back and I began to quickly slap together a sandwich. It wasn't going to be eat and run—but on the run.

"Move aside woman," the first blue-jawed and ugly copper said. If he had left it at that he would have been much happier. But he made the mistake of putting one meaty hand on her shoulder to push her aside.

He had time for a single pained shriek, I heard the unmistakable crackle of breaking bone, before he dropped unconscious onto the carpet. The second policeman was drawing his gun as I laid down the sandwich, but before I could reach him he was laid down by his companion. The waiter fled and Angelina, smiling happily, closed the door behind him. I finished a second sandwich, wrapped them both in a napkin, then added a bottle of ron to my lunchtime arrangements.

"Time for me to leave," I said, bending over the sleeping beauties and touching the backs of their necks with the slaphypo. "I've given them both knockout shots, good for a day at least. We can't have them waking up and identifying you as their assailant. At least not until after the meet at midnight."

I kissed her warmly and a sudden pounding on the door sounded an echo to my osculation.

"Better find another way out," I said and strolled out onto the balcony. Angelina followed nibbling delicately on a drumstick. We were twenty stories up, the wall smooth and unclimbable. No problem at all. "Hold this for a moment, if you please," I said, handing her my luncheon pack.

It was the work of a moment to slip over the edge of the balcony, to hang by my hands, to swing and land lightly on the balcony of the room directly below. Angelina dropped the picnic pack into my waiting grasp and blew me a kiss. Things were going well, very well indeed.

The apartment was fortuitously empty so I seized the opportunity to satisfy my hunger and slake my thirst. I had polished off the last crumb and was nipping delicately at the ron when I heard the key rattle in the door. I belched lightly, reluctantly put down the unfinished bottle, and was flat against the wall behind the door when it opened.

No tourist here! Two men in military uniform, weapons drawn, came into the room. I waited until I was sure there were no more coming before stepping out behind them.

"Looking for someone?" I asked.

They spun about, weapons swinging up, growling with anger. I held my breath and popped the sleep capsule under their noses, then stepped back while they clanked and clattered to the carpet. One of them was about my size which presented me with a very obvious yet still interesting idea.

My only real complaint was that I would have preferred it if the soldier had bathed more often. When I put his uniform on over my beach clothes I had a definite fragrance to remember him by. As neat as his uniform was, his undergarments were a lacework of holes and patches. A soldier's salary could not be very high. But no money had been spared on his equipment. Microradio, ion rifle with a full charge, .50 recoilless sidearm and full refill clips of ammunition. By the time I had put everything into place I looked quite efficiently military. And my skin was tanned to the same color as that of the locals.

"Well done, Jim, well done indeed," I congratulated myself.

"The Stainless Steel Rat strikes again, penetrating where no other dares, insinuating himself into the ferroconcrete wainscoting of society. Moving like a ghost, striking like lightning. Fearless and forceful. Great!"

With my morale heightened by these well-deserved compliments I gave a last adjustment to my uniform and opened the door.

The doorframe exploded beside my face and bullets crashed and screamed around me.

THIS SIDE OF CARD IS FOR ADDRESS

5

I slammed the door shut again and hurled myself aside. Just as another burst of firing stitched a neat row of holes through the paneling of the door where I had been standing.

"This will not do much for the tourist trade," I muttered, as I crawled on my belly to the balcony. Now that I knew that these boys were playing for keeps, I draped the helmet over the gunbarrel and poked it forward cautiously. Quick shots sounded from the adjoining balcony and the helmet jumped and clattered at my feet. Short-tempered. I put it on again and tried to ignore the shining dents.

"You should not be so greedy, James," I said. "You are paying now for your little luncheon break." Harsh words, but true enough—and I deserved them. When I am right, which is very often, I admit it. But when I am wrong I admit that as well. A criminal who tries to fool himself is very quickly an ex-criminal and is either two meters underground or looking out at the sky through the bars in front of his window.

"Moment of contrition has passed. Now—how do you get out of this. Think hard."

I thought. Both my flanks were held by the enemy and time was running out. Time to open a new flank. I hurried into the bathroom, just as automatic fire penetrated the front door once again. The shower seemed the best bet at this time of day. I didn't want to cause any accidents to innocent bystanders. I took out the debonder, switched it on, then quickly ran it in a circle over the bottom of the shower pan.

The molecular debonder has been called a disintegrator ray, which is not true. It does not destroy any material at all. It simply works on the molecular bonds that hold all matter together, lessening their charges for a brief instant. When this happens the binding energy that binds the molecules of matter to each other no longer holds them together. Simple enough, isn't it?

The bottom of the shower pan, and the floor beneath it, fell away and smashed down into the shower of the apartment directly below. As I dropped through after it I heard the apartment door behind me crash open. The wisest thing to do now was to keep moving. I did. Out of the bathroom and into the sitting room where I found a trembling female tourist from our ship. She was frantically punching a number into the phone. She looked up at me and screamed.

"*Caña, caballero, Español, ron!*" I called out hoarsely, exhausting my knowledge of the local language at the same time. She screamed and fainted. Wonderful. I eased the door open a crack; the hall was empty.

It was time for speed, not caution. I went down the hall at a dead run, brushing past a gaggle of tourists, and on into the corridor that led to the service stairs. I always check the layout of a new building when I first arrive and, not for the first time, I was glad that I had this habit. The door to the service stairs was just where I had seen it last and I was about to pull it open when I heard the thunder of running feet inside. They were ahead of me! But the sound began to die away. I took a chance and opened the door a crack. Wide enough to see uniformed backs vanishing down the stairs. Perfect!

I vanished after them.

The sergeant leading the pack shouted encouragement at the soldiers as they ran, stumbling on the stairs in their heavy boots. I scurried down after them, stayed just behind them— then merged with the pack as the stragglers slowed, gasping for breath. We all staggered out on the ground floor in a shambling run to join the other soldiers and police milling about here. It was simplicity itself to work my way out to the edge of the mob, then to slip away between the buildings.

A few minutes later I found myself whistling cheerily as I stowed the uniform and equipment in a bin behind the hotel kitchen. Once this had been done I became a simple tourist again, one of the goggle-eyed horde that milled about and shouted to one another for information about what was going on. Some of the guides and hotel workers were attempting to calm them, but I stayed well away from any of the locals, no matter how innocent they appeared to be. I joined some tourists on the beach, and if I strolled further down the sunny sands than they did, who was to say no? A headland pushed out to form a bay here, and when I walked around it I was safely out of sight of the hotel and all of the disturbance I had so unwittingly caused.

By this time I was pleasantly tired. An easy climb up the bank brought me to the edge of the jungle. I sat down gratefully in the shade of a large tree, out of sight of the beach below, and enjoyed the changing colors of the twilight. The sun dropped into the ocean, without the slightest hiss, and darkness slowly descended. So did I. The grass was soft, the jungle free of tropical insects; my eyes closed and I slept the sleep of the innocent and the just.

It was either the ron or the exercise, or both, for I didn't stir until the rising sun struck color from the sky above. I yawned, stretched—and listened to the rumble of my empty stomach. It was time to return. But before I did, I emptied my pockets of all my illegal equipment and buried the items at the base of a large tree. Then, innocent and unshaven, I made my way back to the hotel complex.

With the same amount of precaution I had used in leaving it. After all I had gone through I did not want to get a hole blown through me by some trigger-happy recruit. The only way to get off this planet was to surrender to the authorities. But I wanted to do that on my own terms.

The restaurant was the ideal place. I approached it under the cover of the ornamental shrubbery, out of sight of the policemen stamping up and down before the entrance, and slipped in through an open window. A few early risers were already tucking into their breakfasts and I intended to do the same. I filled a plate from the buffet, poured a glass of juice and a cup of coffee, and was well into the same before one of the waiters noticed me and did a trembling take. As he hurried off I took my coffee and moved to another table that was closer to the other diners.

"What was all that trouble about yesterday?" I asked an elderly couple who were shoveling down eggs as though the last hen alive had just died.

"Won't tell us, that's what. Not a word," he said between bites. She nodded agreement, never slowing. "Not good enough I told them. Didn't pay my money to watch a gunfight. Money back I told them, next ship out."

Before I could think of a witty answer there was a struggle in the doorway as a half-dozen policemen pushed their way through and ran to my table. Guns pointed.

"If you make a move we fire!" one of them shouted.

"Waiter!" I called out loudly. "Get the manager! Get somebody, quickly! Tell him to come at once!" I sipped my coffee as the uniformed mob pushed close.

"You will come with us," an officer said.

"Why?" I asked quietly, aware of the watching tourists and hotel employees.

Two of the cops grabbed me by the shoulders and pulled me to my feet. I did not resist, though it took a decided effort of will. More men were approaching and I recognized one of them. Our guide.

"Jorge!" I shouted. "What is the meaning of this? Who are these strangely dressed men?"

"They are police," he said, wringing his hands together and looking very unhappy. "They wish to talk to you."

"Fine. They can talk to me right here. I'm a tourist and I have my rights."

There was a good deal of shouting then in Español, backed by the conversational hum of the gathering tourists. Everything was going fine. Jorge turned back to me, looking even more unhappy.

"I'm sorry, I can do nothing. They wish you to go with them."

"Kidnapped!" I shouted. "A poor tourist kidnapped by fake police! Call the government, call the tourist board, call my consul! You'll pay for this—I'll sue this two-bit planet into bankruptcy if you let this happen."

The onlookers murmured in agreement and they might even have let me go if a tall officer had not pushed through the crowd. He was steely of eye and firm of glance, and immediately took charge of the matter.

"Do not worry my good sir, you are not under arrest, goodness no. Release him at once!" The restraining hands dropped away. He smiled and turned to me, and when he spoke it was as much for the benefit of the watching tourists as for mine.

"It seems there was an accident yesterday and these men believe that you witnessed it . . ."

"I didn't see anything. And who are you?"

"My name is Oliveira, Captain Oliveira. I am pleased to hear that you saw nothing. Would you then be kind enough to come with me and tell me what you didn't see. There were innocent victims of the accident and I'm sure that you would want to help them. Don't you?"

His smile was so sincere, his logic so impeccable that now I was beginning to look like the broken cog in the wheels of justice. I was just as reasonable.

"Glad to help. But where are we going? I want to leave a message for my wife."

For an instant there was cold anger beneath Oliveira's warm smile. "To central police headquarters . . ."

"Fine. Hey, you," I waved a waiter over. "As soon as I go I want you to go up and see my wife in twenty-ten. Tell her what happened. Tell her I'll be back for lunch. Do you hear that, folks?" I raised my voice so every tourist within earshot knew what was happening. "I'm going to help these kind policemen in an accident investigation. Maybe they'll tell me what all the noise was about around here yesterday. I'll come back by lunchtime and let you know all about it. Let's go Captain Oliveira."

I moved towards the door so fast that they had to hurry to follow me. I had done what I could; now it was up to the police. If I suffered any unfortunate accidents everyone present would know who was to blame.

There were dark looks and mutterings in tongues as we all jammed into a patrol car. After this it was screaming sirens and screeching tires as we hurtled up the road away from the beach, past the airport and on into the city beyond. Captain Oliveira did not travel with us. I saw him speed ahead in another car. Undoubtedly to prepare a reception for me. But I laugh at fear and danger! I laughed aloud to prove this and the policemen looked at me as though I were mad. Maybe I was—to come here in the first place. But it was a little late for second thoughts. I practiced breathing exercises and relaxing techniques and was feeling very fit indeed when we drove through an open gate and on into a grim-looking courtyard.

What followed was pretty much routine, a routine, that is, that I had experienced far too often before. I was stripped to the skin and my clothes whisked away to be searched. My fair body was x-rayed and a dentist, with a terminal case of garlic breath, examined my teeth closely. Just for a change there were no devices concealed there, or anywhere else on my person. When this ritual was completed I was given a cotton robe and a pair of scuffs to wear. With a stout policeman on each side I was hurried into the presence of Captain Oliveira. All pretense of politeness had vanished. His voice was cold and his gaze penetrating.

"Who are you?" he said.

"A simple tourist abused by your bullies . . ."

"*Cargata!*" he growled, and I memorized the word, sure that it was a bit of local profanity that would come in handy. "You were observed talking to a wanted criminal and were given a message by this person. When you were questioned by an officer performing his duty you assaulted him. When other policemen came to question you about this you assaulted them as well. This is a peaceful world and we will not allow this kind of violence. More police and troops were sent to arrest you before you caused any more violence—but you did assault more men and cause more violence. You will now tell me who you are and what you are doing here—and what the message was you received from the local criminals."

"No," I said firmly, my expression now just as coldly angry as his was. "I came to your miserable planet for a holiday. I was attacked and defended myself. I was a combat marine for a number of years so I know exactly how that should be done." I had had this fact inserted in my identification just in case of circumstances like this one. "I don't know why your thugs attacked me—nor do I care. They tried to kill me and I fought back. I then waited until it was quieter before I reappeared and surrendered. Now you can release me. I have nothing more to say."

"No!" he shouted, losing his temper and hammering his fists on the desk. "You will tell me the truth or I will beat it out of you . . ."

"You're an idiot, Oliveira. All of those tourists know that I am in police custody. Touch one hair of my head and there goes your tourist industry. Forever. Now I am prepared to make a single statement. Just once. And I want a lie detector when I do it . . ."

"That chair you are sitting in is a lie detector. Speak!"

I'm glad I hadn't known that while I was lying! Now all I had to do was watch how I phrased my statement.

"Good. Now, for the record. I was given a book by someone I had never seen before. I have not seen this person since, so I could not have received any information from her. I don't know who she is or why she contacted me. Period. End of statement. Now get my clothes because I am getting out of here."

I stood and faced him in silence. His expression did not change, but I could see an artery throbbing furiously in his temple. He was possessed with anger—but he was smart. He had to kill me or let me go. That was all the choice he had and he knew it. When he finally spoke it was in a low and controlled voice. But I believed every word that he said.

"I'm releasing you. You will be returned to your hotel and you will pack your bags. My men will stay with you. They will take you and your wife to the space terminal to leave on the next flight. You will go away and you will never come back. Because if you *do* return to this planet I will kill you on sight. You are involved in something dirty here. I don't know what it is—nor do I care. Do you understand me?"

"Perfectly, Captain. And I want to leave this planet just as much as you want me to go."

However I didn't add that I wanted to come back just as strongly. The captain and I were going to meet again.

6

Angelina and I had no chance to speak together until we were in deep space. Before that, lowbrowed policemen were thick about us at all times, looking over our shoulders as we packed, then whisking us away as soon as the bags were closed. The departure of a cruise ship was held for over an hour until we arrived. It took off as soon as we were aboard. Once the acceleration was over I poured myself some hundred-proof nerve tonic, then used the detector in the camera to sweep our cabin; it was clear of bugs.

"It's clean," I said. "Did you make the midnight meet?"

"You told me that you were contacted by one of the locals." Angelina's voice was chilled to about four degrees Kelvin. "You forgot to mention that this local was also a highly attractive and concupiscent young woman."

"My love! You wrong me. I saw her for a few moments only. Nothing more!"

"There better be nothing more. I know all about your over-sexed libido, Jim diGriz. Lay one finger on her and I'll cut it off."

"Agreed, not a finger. Now *please* tell me what happened."

"I took the walk along the beach. She was hidden at the edge of the jungle. She called to me, asked me if I had read the note. I repeated the message and let her know that you were otherwise engaged. So she told me the story. Her name is Flavia and she is a member of what she admits is a poorly organized resistance movement. They are powerless to even protest. As fast as they organize they are penetrated and captured. Imprisoned or killed. Their only hope is to make their plight known to the galaxy at large."

"I'm afraid the galaxy already knows—and doesn't really care."

"I neglected to tell her that. She was so happy that I would be taking their message to other worlds. Five pages of it. She was very impressed when I memorized it after reading it once."

"In the dark?"

"Shut up. It was written in luminescent ink. And very depressing reading it made too. One of the reasons that the other planets don't care about politics here is because the government superficially appears to be a democracy. Every four years there is an election for president. The only thing wrong with this arrangement is that the election is rigged and General-President Julio Zapilote always gets reelected. He is serving his forty-first term now . . ."

"He must be two hundred years old!"

"He is. Geriatric treatments. He is backed by a bunch of military thugs who keep the population in line. A typically polarized situation with all the power concentrated in his hands. A few very rich at the top who run everything, with the starving and practically enslaved masses at the bottom. With a small middle class in between."

"That has to change," I said, pacing the cabin and thinking rapidly.

"I agree. But it won't be easy."

"Everything is easy for the man who saved the universe!"

"Twice," she reminded me.

"That's the truth. I am going to go back there . . ."

"Say we. The boys and I need a holiday too."

"We, of course, my love. And your two strapping sons as well. Did Flavia give you any reason why they tried to contact me?"

"The guide, Jorge, told them about you and your interest in the workings of their society."

"Fine. If we have to contact them again we can do it through Jorge. And contact them we will! A man was killed trying to bring me a message about their planet. And having seen the planet I can understand why. I intend to go back there. And in addition I have a score to settle with a certain Captain Oliveira, the one who arrested me."

She frowned murderously. "If he touched a single hair on your head I'll kill him. Painfully."

"Wonderful wife! Don't worry, I'll take care of the captain. You can concentrate on freeing the rest of the planet."

"Sounds like a good idea. Do you have any idea of how you are going to do it?"

"No. But that has never stopped me in the past. We will

equip ourselves and return and I'm sure that I will think of something."

"Shall we invade them? Get a mercenary army together?"

"Something a little more subtle is in order. We'll bore from within, as a stainless steel rat should. And I already have some ideas how we are going to do that!"

Needless to say, the twins were delighted by the idea. James was leading a zoological expedition to capture poisonous specimens on the fog-shrouded, horror-planet Veniola that creeps in its orbit around the ghoulish star Hernia. As soon as word reached him he caged his last specimen and headed home at full blast. He arrived just a little ahead of Bolivar who had been doing research into prison reform. He had been imprisoned in the escape-proof prison on Helior, from which he instantly escaped when my message was smuggled to him. Young appetites always need nourishment, so I waited patiently as they consumed one of their mother's excellent nine-course meals before they joined me in my study.

"There is something about you different, Dad," James said.

"Very observant, brother," Bolivar said. "Seeing as how our dad now has dark skin, black hair and moustache, dark eyes, a new jaw and different cheekbones."

"And also speaks a new language," I said in perfect Español.

"Sounds nice," James said. "Easy to understand, a little like Esperanto."

"By morning you will have splitting headaches and be speaking it yourselves. A few hours with the language indoctrinator will jam it into your skulls."

"Then what? Thanks Mom," Bolivar said added as Angelina brought a tray with filled wine glasses into the room.

"Then we are off to Paraiso-Aqui where they ferment this fine wine." We all sipped and smacked our lips with pleasure. "The name of this world means Paradise Here, and we will see if we can't make that name come true at last."

"How?" Angelina asked, and not for the first time.

"I'll think of something when we are on the spot. Meanwhile I have made plans to return there in style. If you will look at that . . ."

I pressed the button that rolled up the wall, revealing the adjoining workshop. A large and rather battered touring car was revealed.

"Doesn't look like much," the ever-truthful Bolivar said.

"Thank you. That was my intent. It is an exact duplicate of

a car I photographed on Paraiso-Aqui. Resembling the original in every detail . . ."

"But containing a number of details the original never contained!" James said.

"Smart lad. Careful! Don't press any buttons or switch any switches until I have explained how they work. The real vehicles like this on Paraiso-Aqui are powered by something called an infernal combustion engine. It is unbelievably complicated and inefficient. Good sugar cane is wasted to make ethyl alcohol, instead of being used sensibly to produce ron, which is then poured into one end of the engine. Water vapor and poisonous gas come out of the other. Horrible. Therefore our car is powered by a small atomic engine. This also energizes the lasers built into the headlights, powers the gun positions, works the radar to aim the mortars. You know the sort of things."

"We certainly do!" Angelina said, smiling happily. "What is the next step?"

"Final preparations. In two days we will all be rested and refreshed, darker of skin and hair, and speaking Español with a native fluency. A Special Corps spacer, with all of the latest electronic detection and avoidance gear, will pick up us and our car and transfer us to Paraiso-Aqui. They will leave us there, alone and defenseless . . ."

"Hardly!" Bolivar said.

". . . thousands of light-years from the nearest friendly planet. Four lost souls against an entire world. Four friendless people pitted against the might of a planet-wide dictatorship. I feel sorry for them . . ."

"Do you mean the dictatorship, not us?" Angelina asked.

"Of course! The wine then. We drink to their downfall and the beginning of a new life for Paraiso-Aqui."

7

Even I, hardened by a thousand battles and even more close calls, had to admit that I experienced a sudden stab of the old *angst* when I watched the Corps battle cruiser lift up silently into the night. It is one thing to sit in your own home, glass in hand, and brag about how great you are. It is quite another thing altogether to be dumped on an inhospitable planet with all your loved ones and every man's hand turned against you. Were we doomed? If so I was responsible.

"Well Dad . . ." Bolivar said.

". . . the fun's about to begin!" James added, finishing his twin's sentence for him. They laughed together and slapped me on the back, which staggered me a bit and also dragged me out of my fit of depression. We could do it! We *would* do it!

"You're absolutely right, boys. Here we go!"

James opened the rear door of the touring car for his mother, while Bolivar, decked out in chauffeur's uniform, climbed into the front seat and started the engine. It was a cloudless night and the starlight was bright enough for us to see our way. I joined Angelina while James climbed into the front seat beside his brother. He wore the white suit and black string tie of a minor functionary. While Angelina and I were dressed in the finery of the wealthy, copied faithfully from photographs taken from the guide books. Bolivar put on dark glasses, kicked the car into gear, and we shot off into the darkness.

Of course his glasses were sensitive to ultraviolet. And the headlights, while apparently turned off, were nevertheless radiating great beams of ultraviolet light. It was disconcerting, yet strangely exciting, to hurtle through the night like this.

"The ground here is hard stone all the way, Dad," Bolivar said. "Just the way you planned. We'll leave no tracks, just in case the authorities saw the ship land and come to investigate. And the road is right ahead. Empty. Hold on, it's going to be bumpy going across the shoulder."

We slithered and joggled our way up onto the road, which turned out to be smooth and well-paved. The car picked up speed as it hurtled along in darkness through the night.

"Turn on the lights after we get around the next bend," I said. "We will then become legitimate citizenry out for a spin."

"How far do you want us to spin?" he asked.

"As far as the coast. If we get there early we'll rest a bit, then go on after dawn. I don't want to reach the resort until after daylight. Once there we'll find some place for breakfast before we proceed with the next step of the plan."

We had the road to ourselves for the most part. An occasional car passed in the opposite direction, but there were no signs of any alarm. I took a bottle of champagne from the cooler and Angelina and I drank a toast to success. I then switched the television on to a recorded symphony and we zoomed on through the night, if not in the lap of luxury at least in the car of content. By maintaining a stately and steady speed we reached the coast just as day was breaking, then turned onto the road to the resort. They were early risers here and already the peasantry were on their way to the fields. They drew aside at our approach, bowing and saluting, which attentions we ignored in the proper manner. Warm sunlight sparkled on the water as we drove majestically along the waterfront.

"There," Angelina said. "The outdoor restaurant right on the shore. The waiters are setting the tables. It looks perfect."

"As indeed it is. Bolivar, let us off there, park the car where we can keep an eye on it, then take a table at an appropriate distance."

There is nothing like being rich in a place where everyone else is poor. It helps the service no end. Our arrival was noted and the restaurant manager himself hurried out.

"Welcome, welcome Your Honor and Lady!" he said, opening the car door himself. "A table, yes, this one, at your service. Your slightest wish is my command."

"A light for my cigar," I sneered, taking a long black cheroot from my case. Three waiters fought for the privilege of lighting it; tiny flames flared. I puffed smoke, dropped into a chair, and pushed my wide-brimmed hat back on my head. Angelina sat down demurely opposite me.

"This is the life," I sighed.

"You're a born fascist," Angelina said under her breath. "We are here to save these people from being trampled under, not to glory in the trampling ourselves."

"I know. But that doesn't mean we can't enjoy ourselves before the trampling has to stop. Just because we're on a sinking ship it doesn't mean we have to travel in steerage. First class all the way! And about time too," I added, taking the menu from the trembling waiter.

Some while later, stomach happily full, I was enjoying a cigar with my third cup of rich black coffee, looking out casually at the passing parade. Then I dropped my cigar onto the ground and snapped my fingers in James's direction. As he came hurrying over, radiating fearful employee in a satisfactory manner, I took out a fresh cheroot.

"Light this!" I ordered, then spoke in a quieter voice when he bent over. "When you turn around take a look at the man in the green shirt talking to the three fat tourists. Our luck is holding because that is Jorge, our contact. Follow him. Find out where he goes."

"No trouble, Papa. He'll never know he's being tailed."

As he turned away, Angelina leaned close and said, "Dear one, if you now will glance to your right you will see that trouble is on the way."

I glanced—and indeed it was on the way. Two sordid types, dressed in plain clothes but radiating authority, had stopped to talk to the young couple sitting at the first table. The diners produced papers which the thugs looked through carefully. They were obviously checking for identification. Which posed an interesting problem for us since we didn't have any.

"Angelina," I said as I snapped my fingers for the waiter, "you are most observant. Get Bolivar and go to the car while I pay up here. Pick me up at the curb."

The waiters were fast but the police thugs were even faster. They went by the next two tables, obviously occupied by off-planet tourists, and approached me just as I was throwing handfuls of money onto the bill.

"If you please, your honor, you have identification papers?" the smaller and slimmer one said.

I looked him up and down in slow and arrogant silence, waiting until he broke into a cold sweat before I spoke.

"Of course I have identification papers." I turned away and stepped to the curb as the touring car rolled ponderously up. It might have worked. It didn't this time. His voice quavered tremulously behind me.

"Would you be so kind as to show them to me, if you please."

The car was close—but not close enough. I turned back and fixed him with a basilisk gaze. "What is your name?" I growled.

"Viladelmas Pujol, your eminence . . ."

"I'll say this just once, Pujol. I do not talk to policemen on the street. Nor do I show them papers. Leave me."

He turned away instantly, but his large partner was made of sterner—or stupider—stuff.

"We will be pleased to accompany you to the Commissioner of Police, your excellency. He will be most happy to welcome you to our city."

It was time to think fast. This repulsive little scene had been going on for far too long and would draw attention soon. There was no point in attempting to flee in the car; they could see its registration number and could identify us. So I thought fast and, within a split second, devised a highly satisfactory plan just as the car pulled up and stopped beside us.

"How very kind of you to offer." I smiled and they relaxed and smiled as well, with some relief. "As a stranger here I do not know my way. So you will accompany me in my luxurious vehicle and instruct my driver."

"Thank you! Thank you!"

It was all smiles and good will as we climbed in; I'm sure they would have kissed my hand had I but extended it. Bolivar pressed the proper button and the jump seats dropped down into position. They dropped their fat rumps gingerly onto the hand-tooled leather, facing us, as the car started forward smoothly.

"Kindly instruct my driver," I said, then turned to Angelina. "These kind policemen are escorting us to meet their Commissioner who wishes to greet us."

"Charming," she said, lifting one eyebrow delicately.

"Straight ahead, then right at the third turning," Pujol said.

"All friends together," I said, smiling at them and they beamed back with pleasure. "Or as the great poet wrote, 'Kiam me kalkulos al tri, vi endormigos vian malbonulon kaj mi endormigos mian.'" Which as any first year Esperanto student knows means "When I count to three, you put your thug to sleep and I'll take care of mine."

"I'm not much on poetry, excellency," Pujol said.

"Then I'll teach you some right now. It's as easy as one, two, three . . ."

I leaned over and took Pujol by the throat and squeezed hard. He bulged his eyes, gaped, thrashed a bit, then collapsed. Angelina, who dislikes police of any kind, had been more dramatic. She had extended one shapely leg and kicked the big one in the stomach. When he had folded forward, a quick chop to the exposed nape of his neck had dropped him at her feet.

"Neatly done, Mom and Dad," Bolivar said, looking in the rearview mirror. "Not a soul in the street noticed. And I've just gone by the third turning."

"Very good. Just drive on along the coast while we figure out what to do with them."

"Cut their throats, wire boulders to their ankles, dump them into the sea," Angelina said, smiling cheerfully.

"No, darling," I said, patting her graceful hand, "you are reformed, remember? No more maiming or slaughter . . ."

"That doesn't apply to the police!"

"Yes, dearest, to the police as well." She sat back in her corner muttering darkly, while I explained what I had in mind. "When I spoke of figuring out what to do with them, I simply meant where we would leave them after they have each been given a shot of amnesial. A drug which, as you undoubtedly know, wipes out all memory of events that took place up to twenty hours before the injection."

"Strychnine works faster."

"It does, my pet, but it is far more permanent."

"Look, Dad, there's a side road ahead," Bolivar said. "It appears to lead up towards the jungle."

"Perfect. Go that way while I give them the shots."

Since mayhem had been ruled out, Angelina would have nothing to do with the arrangements. I slipped out the medkit and took care of everything myself. Bolivar found an unpaved farm track leading off among the trees and backed into it. We slipped the sleeping simpletons under some thick bushes and left, driving back along the same route. James was waiting near the restaurant and climbed into the front seat.

"Been joyriding?" he asked.

"Getting rid of some nosy cops," I told him. "What happened to Jorge?"

"I followed him to a bar and was drinking nearby when he told his friends how he had been up all night at a tourist party and was now going to go to bed."

"Where he is now—and you know where it is?"

"Right the first time, Dad. And I imagine you would like to disturb his beauty sleep. I'll show you the way."

I went in alone, picking the front door lock with a single dextrous twitch of my fingers. I've done this sort of thing so often before that I had to stifle a yawn. You're a real pro, Jim, I told myself as I tiptoed in silence across the darkened room. Pride goeth before a fall. Jorge either had ears like a cat, was an incredibly light sleeper—or there was a silent alarm attached to the front door. But whatever it was didn't matter. The result did.

The lights came on just as I was halfway across the room. Jorge stood in the doorway to the bedroom aiming a large and nasty-looking pistol at me.

"Say a farewell prayer, spy," he said coldly. "For I am about to kill you."

8

"Don't shoot, Jorge! I'm a friend . . ."

"Who skulks in like a thief in the night?"

"In the day, full daylight out. And I came this way because I didn't want to be seen. I'm one of the good guys, like you, and like Flavia . . ."

That almost got me killed. "What do you know of Flavia?" He shouted, and I swear the knuckle on his trigger finger whitened with the strain. I put a little drama into the situation by dropping to my knees and spreading my arms wide in supplication.

"Hear me out, brave Jorge! I come from the other planets where your message was received. The one you gave to the tourist and his wife who were kicked off your fair world."

"How do you know about that?" The gun muzzle lowered slightly. I stood up, brushed off my knees, then went to sit on his couch.

"I know—because I am that tourist. A little disguised outside, but still the same within."

"I do not believe you. You could be a police spy."

"Right. I could be anything. But I'm not and I can prove it. I know things no one else could possibly know. Like I know that it was my wife who met Flavia on the beach, where Flavia gave her a five-page message for help, which she memorized right on the spot. Which she later told to me, which I memorized too, which I will recite for you."

And I did, all five pages of it. And as I droned on and on the gun sank lower and lower until, when I finished, he put it aside.

"I believe you now," he said. "For I wrote that message and only Flavia has seen it." He rushed forward, eyes flashing, and pulled me to my feet and embraced me, then kissed me warmly on both cheeks. He needed a shave.

"Yes, well, I'm glad we agree at last," I said, pulling myself free. "Always happy to be of help."

"I still find it hard to believe," he waxed. "We have always failed in the past to get aid from outside. Some months ago we managed to smuggle one of our members out on a tourist ship, but we have heard nothing of him since."

"Was he small, dark and with a crooked nose?"

"He was. But how did you know . . .?"

"It is my sad duty to inform you that he is dead. Undoubtedly murderd by police agents."

"Poor Hector, he was such a brave man. He was sure that he would be able to contact the legendary Rat of Steel, who might condescend to help us . . ."

Jorge's voice ran out like a broken recording machine and his eyes bulged interestingly from his head. I looked down humbly at my nails, then buffed them on my lapel. He gurgled.

"You aren't . . . you can't be . . ."

"Happily for your sake—I am! I am known by many names throughout the worlds. De rat van roestvrij staal, Ratinox, die Edelstahlratte, El Escurridizo, even un criminale al nichel-cromo. At your service. Now tell me about your setup here, and what your plans are."

"Simply and depressingly stated. We have no plans and are in a state of disarray. The secret police are too efficient. All resistance organizations are penetrated and destroyed even as they are formed. Ours is a new organization and already Flavia is known and in hiding. Since I see many tourists it was she who devised the plan to seek help from off our planet. I am ashamed, we are so feeble."

"Best news ever. Gives me a free hand. Do you have any idea if there are others with like feelings?"

"All of the peasants would like to kill President Zapilote and his army of secret police, the Ultimados as they are called. But they are powerless. The power is in the hands of the rich and the middle class, and they are the ones who support Zapilote all the way. Of course he is disliked by many of the old nobility who lost power when he took over, but they are not organized in any way."

I had the glimmerings of an idea. "Nobility? Tell me more about them."

"There is little to be said. It is from their ranks that I so shamefully come. I have an unimpressive title, of no importance. It is because of the title that I am trusted to meet with the tourists. Rank still has a few small privileges. Until that swine Zapilote appeared on the scene we had a peaceful monarchy on this planet. Admittedly it was inefficient and didn't work very well, but people had enough to eat and there was no murder or torture. But there was just enough unrest so that people listened when Zapilote began preaching his liberty and equality for all. It sounded good—but he meant nothing that he said. It was just words to him. But enough people had faith in him so that the democratic movement spread until even the nobility began to think that it was a good idea. The first elections were held and Zapilote became president. By the time he was up for re-election he had all of the corrupt generals on his side, as well as his secret police. With the help of the military and his Ultimados that election was rigged, and every one since then, every four years. Though apparently he will soon be up for election again he is in reality General-President for life."

The idea that had been scratching away at my subconscious broke through at last and I shouted aloud with joy.

"Oh no, he's not! This planet is going to see an election like it has never seen before!"

"What do you mean?"

"We are going to find one of the old nobility who can be trusted, who is, hopefully, honest enough to want to run for office. Then we will make him a candidate for president."

"But the election will be rigged!"

"You had better believe that. Rigged by me! I'll teach these backwater-planet election-riggers a thing or two about crooked politics. We'll win in a landslide."

"Can it be done?"

"Just watch. But it is up to you to find us a decent candidate."

He rubbed his jaw and frowned. "I must think."

"Why don't we lubricate the thought processes with some ron?"

"Wonderful. I have aged ron here that is too good for the tourists, if you will excuse my saying so, that you might enjoy."

I certainly did. I smacked and sipped and made yum-yum noises and we toasted each other and the coming new day and finally got back to work.

"The best people are those who live farthest from the cities," Jorge said, alcohol and ron having worked their wonders upon his brain, which was now churning away at a great rate. "Deep in the interior of this continent there are the large estates where they raise coffee and wheat and bizcocho berries. The peasants who work there are happy, the overseers kind, the nobility fair. As long as they supply food to the cities and stay out of politics, why Zapilote lets them alone."

"Do you know any of these people?"

"I know all of them, of course, since we are all related."

"Can you think of any one of them might help us out?"

"Just one. Gonzales de Torres, the Marquez de la Rosa. He is just, honest, fair, upright, handsome, courageous and hates Zapilote."

"He can't be all bad. How well do you know him?"

"He is a third cousin four times removed on my mother's side. I see him at funerals and weddings and things like that. But I know all about him. There are no secrets in the aristocracy."

"I have a feeling he is our man. How do we get in touch with him?"

"We must obtain a car . . ."

"Already done. Will you come with us?"

"I dare not leave my job! It would be too suspicious. But Flavia could guide you. I will give her a message. She will be safer away from this place."

I took a last guzzle of the ron and placed the glass reluctantly back on the table. "Then it's all set. I'll take my troops for a ride in the country where we will have a picnic and a siesta. By this time it will be after dark and you will tell me where and when we are to pick her up."

"It will take time to locate her—and I must work today. But if you will come to this building at midnight I will be outside. I will take you to her."

"As good as done."

I started to leave then turned back and pointed to the dust-shrouded bottle of vintage ron. "Once they are opened these ancient beverages tend to spoil. You wouldn't like me to take care of that for you?"

"Take it, I beg you," he said pressing the bottle upon me. "I have more, I will bring many bottles with me tonight when we meet."

"There are advantages to this planet never mentioned in the tourist brochures. Aged ron and rigged elections. Why this place is a paradise indeed!"

9

"Sounds like a great plan, Dad," the twins said in enthusiastic chorus.

"It would be a lot greater if that foxy Flavia weren't coming along with us," Angelina sniffed.

I took a delicate sip of the aged ron and waved my hand in airy dismissal. "Dear wife, my philandering days are long past—even if they only existed in your deliciously suspicious mind. I have eyes for no other! Even the fair Flavia."

Angelina arched her eyebrows at my words, either in disbelief, or appreciation, and I did not question her as to which. Life was quiet and restful at the moment and I intended to savor every fleeting instant. Because it was sure to get very busy in the near future. This was the lull before the storm, the girding of loins before the conflict. We sat in the clearing in the forest, high in the hills above the coast, delightfully full after our rustic picnic. Empty dishes were scattered around us; the sun was dropping, as was the level in the ron bottle. James was dozing, Bolivar tinkering with the car; I lay with my head in Angelina's lap very much at peace with the world.

"This is the life," I sighed. "Maybe I ought to retire to some restful planet like this where we can while away our declining years in the sunlight . . ."

"Nonsense," Angelina said in her most practical voice. "You would be bored to exasperation in less than a day. The only reason you are enjoying yourself now is because you are about to go into action—and you are also half-bombed on that antique ron you have been knocking back all day."

"You slight me! I'm as sober as a octogenarian teetotaler. I can recite pi to twenty decimal places."

"Say she sells sea shells."

"See shells she sells."

"Wonderful!" She stood up suddenly and my head thudded

44

to the ground. "Time we got going. James, carry your father to the car if he is unable to walk."

James opened a conspiratorial eye and winked at me. I winked back and rolled over. Then did a quick fifty push-ups to start the blood flowing again. And instantly regretted it as flowing blood started a wicked hammering in my head. This ron was potent stuff. I finished the last dregs in the bottle and hurled it from me, swearing off it for life. Or at least until tomorrow.

Within short moments we were ready for the road again. James had cleared away the debris and Angelina slipped the soiled dishes back into the picnic basket—through the cleaner slot in the lid where supersonics blasted away every remaining trace of food.

I don't remember much about the return journey since I managed to sleep most of the way. Harboring my energies, not sleeping off a drunk as Angelina so humorously suggested. Her dainty elbow in my ribs stirred me to life as we swung by Jorge's apartment. He was waiting in the shadows, darting forward as we stopped and hurling himself in beside us.

"Drive on! Quickly!" he gasped, which Bolivar of course did. "Tragedy has struck! We are lost! Flavia has been captured by the Ultimados!"

"When did this happen?" I asked.

"Just a few minutes ago. I had the call just as I was leaving. A carload of them attacked the farm where she was staying."

"Is this farm far away?"

"Not very far—a half an hour's drive perhaps."

"Then we can cut them off before they bring her in."

"Yes—it is possible!" Enthusiasm replaced despair. "Turn left here, quickly. There is only the single road. But I must warn you, they are heavily armed and dangerous."

Jorge looked around at us as though we were mad, as we all burst out laughing at once. Then fell back into our seats as Bolivar gunned the car to roaring life. Armed and dangerous indeed!

It took us less than five minutes to reach the road that led down from the plateau. Hopefully we were ahead of the heavies. I stood up in the back seat and surveyed the scene for long seconds, working out a plan.

"Right," I said pointing at James. "Dig out a full-size debonder and some needle guns. Everyone out of the car.

Bolivar, take it back down the road out of sight. Angelina, you are going to be the bait in the trap."

"How thoughtful!"

As the car thundered away I pointed my flashlight at a large tree that hung over the road. "Use the debonder to drop that tree right across the road . . ." I tilted my head as I heard the sound of a distant car. "And quickly, since I can hear them coming."

We could see the advancing headlights as we took up our positions of concealment on both sides of the road. Angelina lay sprawled beside the tree, her legs under the trunk as though trapped. The headlights grew brighter, sending swooping beams through the trees, then the car was around the bend with the downed tree directly before it. Brakes squealed and for one horrified moment I thought the thing would hit Angelina. But it shuddered to a stop in time, and she waved an arm feebly and called out for help.

And that's all there was to it. The driver emerged and while his door was open there was the slight rustle of the needle guns firing. Powerful electromagnetic fields hurled out the tiny slivers of steel. Each one tipped with a powerful sleeping drug. The driver folded down neatly onto the road as I jumped forward, flashlight in one hand, gun ready in the other.

My precautions were not needed. The car was filled with the gross and snoring forms of the secret policemen. And, as a measure of our marksmanship, a frightened and conscious Flavia sat in their midst.

"You have been saved," I said taking her hand and helping her from the car. And dropping the hand quickly as my wife appeared, brushing dust from her skirt and firing up the furnaces in her eyes. Jorge took over where I left off, not only taking the abandoned hand but kissing it passionately. He was a great one for kissing was Jorge.

"Other than the fact they almost ran me down it was a satisfactory operation," Angelina said. "All we have to do now is put the driver back into the car with a thermite grenade in his lap."

I sighed and gave her hand a good kissing, a la Jorge, since it seemed a nice thing to do. "I died a thousand deaths while the ancient brakes on this vehicle labored to do their job. Next time I lie under the tree and you shoot the Ultimados. James, Bolivar, would you be so kind as to lay these sleeping uglies out of sight in the woods. Please help yourself to what you might need from their pockets. Jorge—that's it, let her hand dry off for a minute—can you drive this car?"

"Of course! Do you think I am a peasant?"

"Never! Sorry. Can you think of a place to drive it to where it won't be found for awhile?"

"Of course. A nice high cliff above the bay where it will hurtle down into the sea and rest there for eternity."

"I think that will be long enough. So that is your job. Yes, that's right, a few last quick kisses for Flavia's hand and you can take off."

We all waved as the police car rocketed away. Flavia turned to face us and I noticed for the first time that one eye was half-closed and she had bruises on her face.

"I'll get the medkit," Angelina said. "And if I had known that they had worked you over—those Ultimados would be having a far longer sleep."

"I can find no way to thank you," Flavia said, with feeling. "Not only for saving me, but for what you plan to do. Jorge told me everything. Can you do all that you say?"

"He can do anything," Angelina replied, applying antiseptic cream. "With a few certain exceptions as long as I'm around."

"All finished, Dad," Bolivar said, emerging from the woods with an armload of clothing. James was behind him, laden with shoes. "We saw what they did to this young lady so we figured it would be nice if they had to walk back to town naked and barefoot."

"Most considerate. Flavia, these are our sons, James and Bolivar."

They shook hands enthusiastically, while Angelina patted my arm and smiled. "Love at first sight, I can tell by the way they crinkle their eyes. Now shouldn't we get moving?"

We got. Climbing up the road to the plateau, then turning onto the main highway, following Flavia's instructions.

"Once we get into the interior we will be safe, for the Ultimados only dare venture there in armed convoys. But there will be immense difficulties in penetrating the Barrier."

"What is that?" I asked.

"It goes right across the continent and is impossible to get past except at the guard stations. Barbed wire, layers of it, electrified steel mesh fence with poison barbs in the top, concrete walls, mines, detectors of all kinds. Completely impassable."

"Sounds easy enough to get by," Angelina said. "Jim, open another bottle of that nice champagne to settle our nerves while you work out a plan."

Flavia sat on the jump seat sipping daintily at her wine. I barely tasted mine; there had been enough drinking for one day.

"Tell me about the guard stations," I said.

"They are small forts that span the road, which is then completely sealed to passage by double steel gates. Many troops are stationed in the forts and they have heavy weapons of all kinds. In order to pass you must have proper identification. And everything is searched. We will never get by."

"Never," Angelina said firmly, "is a word that our family does not contain in its vocabulary. What do you think, Jim? The barrier or the guard station?"

"The station, of course. It is easier to deal with people than trying to blast our way through all that concrete and hardware. How much further do we have to go?"

Flavia looked out at the next signpost caught by the beam of our headlights. "Two hundred kilometers, perhaps a little more."

"Did you hear that, James?"

"Got it."

"Log it then, so you can turn on the radar about forty Ks out. You should get a good image. Stop when you're ten Ks short of the target and we'll go to action stations."

I could see from her expression that Flavia thought we were mad. Rich tourists in an old car—about to take on the cream of the army. She, as well as they, had a few surprises in store. I sipped a little more champagne as I went over the details of the plan in my head.

"There it is," James said some time later as Bolivar drew the car over onto the shoulder of the road. "You don't even need the radar screen."

How right he was. The twinkling lights of the Barrier stretched out of sight in both directions. While directly ahead was the floodlit bulk of the guard station. It looked ominous and impregnable. I could see Flavia shiver and I wondered if I shouldn't do a little shivering myself. Never! This world was mine for the taking. Zapilote was doomed. We could not flinch back from the first challenge.

"Now hear this," I ordered, slipping a case from under the seat. "These nose plugs will keep you awake while everyone else is being gassed to sleep. Angelina, kindly explain their use to our guide before we advance. Bolivar, close the top. James, arm the gas jets."

There was a smooth whirring as the armored steel top of the open car slid into place. I nodded approval. "We'll do a dry run on the windows. James, you will close them when I say *now!*" There was an echoing thud as all of the windows slammed shut in a fraction of a second. "Good. Now switch me control of the laser cannon. Keep the recoilless cannon armed up there in case the barrier is too thick for the laser."

A control box popped out of the arm rest at my side and I touched the buttons and checked the meters.

"That's it then. Any questions?"

"Just one," James said. "When do we eat?"

"After we get through. Any other questions? Possibly some of a more earth-shaking nature? Good. Then here we go."

The engine rumbled with power as we slid forward to the attack.

10

Of course it was a very slow attack. The longer it took them to discover our nasty intentions the better our chances of success. So we rolled into battle with stately majesty as I broke out another bottle of champagne and labored over the cork. I was still struggling with it as we slowed and stopped before the riveted steel gate. Floodlights burned down and gun muzzles poked out of slits in the stone wall.

"Open, I say, open!" I shouted leaning out of the window. "What do you low-born accumulations of sheep-droppings think you are doing keeping me waiting like this? Driver, sound the horn and wake these idiots up."

The horn sounded, really not a horn but a recording of a steam calliope at full blast. My ears hurt, but I waved the champagne bottle with success as the portal ground slowly upwards. We rolled forward into the fortress to stop before the second sealed gate. I tried to ignore the fact that the first one had closed behind us as I concentrated on the cork. It came out with a resounding pop and Angelina cheered and held out her glass to be refilled. Both boys extended their glasses back for filling and all of us ignored the armed soldiers who were pouring out of the guard room. Out of the corner of my eye I saw Angelina plant an elbow in Flavia's rib to encourage her to get into the act as well. I filled her glass and returned it to her.

"Your papers, at once," an officer ordered, pushing through the troops who stared, goggle-eyed, at our aristocratic excesses.

"Silence, knave, when in the company of your betters," I shouted, sloshing champagne as I gesticulated broadly. "Open the portal, then be gone!"

"Your identification, please," he asked again, a little more humbly now in the presence of his superiors. He was at the open window, looking in, and I saw his eyes widen as he saw Flavia. Recognized! He opened his mouth to shout a command and I hurled the glassful of champagne between his gaping teeth.

"Windows! Gas!" I ordered.

As the windows slammed shut a flood of gas poured from the vents on the car. The officer slid out of sight and his soldiers dropped around him in silent heaps. As the last one fell I hit the switch on the laser gun.

The ruby ray lashed out spectacularly; sparks flew in all directions. And the steel door glowed a nice red color.

"Not too impressive," Angelina said.

"The metal is too thick. James, the cannon. Hit it at the top . . ."

The long hood of the car split open and an ugly, gray muzzle heaved up into firing position. The exploding roar of the recoilless 105 cannon was deafening in that enclosed space. Even inside the insulated car we clutched our ears as the armor-piercing shells tore through the steel. It was like being inside a giant bell with our heads as clappers. The door ahead of us buckled and shook—then collapsed outward with gathering speed and crashed down into the roadway.

Machine-gun bullets crashed and starred the window by my face and clattered like deadly hail off the armored roof, as more soldiers poured out of the doorway. They fired as they came—then collapsed as they walked into the pool of sleeping gas.

"Get us out of here!" I shouted, hardly able to hear myself with the ringing in my ears. *"Wait!"*

One of the soldiers had staggered forward, still shooting as he dropped onto the hood of the car. His sprawled body slid slowly backward and disappeared from sight. If we moved we would run him down.

I had the door open even as I shouted, diving out, stumbling over the thick-piled slumbering troops. One of them had fallen with his arm under the car; I kicked it back. Then I had the soldier in front of the car by the boots and dragged him aside.

As I jumped for the car I had a sudden glimpse of another soldier in a gas mask, raising a gun. It fired, and pain tore through my shoulder spinning me about, knocking me down.

Things became a little hazy then. I tried to stand but only thrashed a bit without moving. Through a blur I saw James standing over me firing a needle gun, then dropping it and grabbing me up. Pushing me headlong into the car. Though I wanted to see what was going on my eyes were closed for some reason. The car surged forward, there were more loud explosions, we bumped and bounced horribly as we rode down the remains of the gate. After that—the bliss of unconsciousness.

When I opened my eyes the first thing I saw was Angelina's fair face. Which is a very nice thing to see at any time, but was particularly welcome at this moment. I started to talk, but started coughing instead. She held a glass of water to my lips, which I gulped at eagerly. She moved aside as she sat the glass down and I found myself looking up at the blue sky. Which was a relief. Far better than a sordid prison ceiling. The water had washed away my speech impediment and I did much better on my second try.

"Mind if I ask how it went?"

"Very well indeed, despite your foolish heroics." But she was smiling as she said this and, could it be true?, was there the tiniest tear in the corner of her eye? I found that her free hand was in mine and I gave it a feeble squeeze and the smile broadened.

"The resistance petered out as the gas seeped through the building. A few soldiers managed to put on gas masks, but the needle guns got them. We went through the gate and straight down the road and it is a good thing the car is armor-plated. There are some really impressive dents in the rear. Some of their cars followed us for awhile, but we left the main road and blew up a bridge and that took care of that. We haven't heard or seen them since. After that we took to the hills and the minor roads, then found this glade and stopped for a rest. As you can see the car and tents are hidden under the trees and all is fine. Except for your arm, which has a very neat entrance wound in your biceps, a nasty exit wound in your triceps and what appears to be a nick on your humerus."

"I don't feel a thing."

"Nor should you, being pumped full of drugs."

I writhed a bit and she helped me sit up, plumping the pillows behind me. I was lying on one of the sleeping bags that had been spread in a row beneath the tall pine trees. The twins were sound asleep, as was Flavia. It was an incredibly peaceful scene, the only sound the boughs above being rustled by the gentle breeze. I was facing downhill across a grassy clearing, looking towards the hills and mountains beyond.

"Have you had any sleep at all?" I asked.

"Someone had to stand watch."

"That's my job now. Get some rest."

She started to protest, but she was a good soldier. There was no reason for her to stay awake. She bent over and kissed me warmly, fussed with the water jar and medications on the folding table at my side, then retired to her own sleeping bag.

The drugs had given me a good case of flannel mouth and I quickly drained the water jug. The silence was so absolute that I could hear birds calling far down the slope. When I stood up I felt a little wobbly, but otherwise all right. As I passed Bolivar his eyes opened and he looked up at me. I gave him the ringed thumb and forefinger gesture that means everything is fine, then touched my finger to my lips. He nodded and closed his eyes again. The car was tucked away far back under the trees. When I looked in I saw that the security alarm was activated, as was the radar. If anything bigger than a bird moved in our direction the alarm would be sounded; one of the boys undoubtedly had the repeater tucked in with him. I had a warm feeling of happiness, knowing that my mob could well take care of themselves under any circumstance.

There was a container of water chilling in the fridge; also a number of bottles of beer. That was more like it! I struggled the top off a beaded bottle and gurgled greedily. Then clutched it by the neck as a makeshift weapon when I heard footsteps moving outside the car. Flavia appeared so I relaxed and drank a bit more.

"You are the only person who could have brought us here," she said. "I thank you from the bottom of my heart."

"Nothing at all. I do it twice a week sometimes. And remember, I had some skilled help."

"I must confess I thought your plan insane when Jorge told me. I never believed that you could possibly win an election against Zapilote. Now I apologize for that doubt. I not only believe that you can accomplish what you say—but I want you to do it. Do you know why?"

"Sorry. Head's still a bit thick. No good at guessing games."

She came forward, stopping no more than an arm's length away. And she was indeed remarkably beautiful. Eyes you could drown in. Lips red and full . . . I sighed and drained the bottle and sat back on the seat to keep my distance from those eyes. She stood there, most serious and radiant, with her hands clasped before the fullness of her bosom.

"I want you to succeed because you are a man of utmost honor. I believe that truly."

"I believe that I am a crook, though I thank you for the kind words. Though the police of a hundred planets probably wouldn't agree with you."

"I do not understand you—but I believe in you. Tell me. Why did you leave the safety of the car and risk being killed?"

"Nothing else I could do. That soldier was under the wheels. He would have been killed when we drove ahead."

"But you risked everything, everyone, for that man's life. How could one man's life be so important?"

"You've just said it yourself. What else is there more important than one person's life? That is all he is ever going to have. All that any of us will ever have. One single shot at existence, with nothing before and nothing to come. What you see is what you get. That's all there is, there ain't no more."

She shook her head. "But my religion tells of the afterlife . . ."

"Good for you. I hope you enjoy the theology. I never knock another man's beliefs, and in turn I expect to be respected for mine. Stated very simply, I face reality and admit that not only isn't there anyone at home upstairs—there isn't even any upstairs. I have one life and I intend to make the most of it. Therefore it follows naturally that if I firmly believe this, why then I cannot deprive another person of their turn at existence. Only the very self-assured political and religious zealots kill people in order to save them. Live and let live, I say. Help the good guys and kick out the bad."

"Well spoken, Dad," Bolivar said, appearing behind Flavia. "Now isn't it time you got some rest? I'll take over the guard."

"Thanks. I'm beginning to think that's not a bad idea at all." He nodded agreement but was looking at Flavia instead of me, and she was returning the look with equal intensity. "Well, I think I'll just totter off. Flavia, if you're not sleepy, why don't you talk to Bolivar. I'm sure he has a lot of questions to ask you about this planet."

They were nodding enthusiastically at the idea when I made my exit. I was nodding to myself as well. Feeling suddenly, well, not exactly old or past it, but definitely as though my generation was being supplanted. Must have been the depressing effect of the drugs or my little religious lecture.

"Brace yourself, Jim, and think strong thoughts!" I muttered to myself as I dropped gratefully back onto the sleeping bag. "You are the planetary savior and they will build statues of you."

Which wasn't too bad a thought and I fell asleep with a smile on my lips.

11

By late afternoon all of the troops were awake and growling for food. My arm was throbbing and felt decidedly uncomfortable. I weighed the relief of dope against a clear head and settled for a clear head. Plans had to be made and a number of alternate courses were already presenting themselves for examination. I shoveled down reconstituted powdered eggs mixed with rehydrated dehydrated bacon, quickly washing the stuff out of sight with caffein condensate. And silently resolved to give more thought to the rations next time we took a trip like this. By the time the plates had been scraped clean my decisions had been made.

"Bolivar, we go to work," I called out magisterially. Was it with some reluctance that he tore himself away from the undisputably charming company of Flavia? Ah youth, youth! "Would you be so kind as to unlimber the large box labeled Top Secret that you will find in the rear compartment."

"Hooray! It's about time we found out what was in there."

The others gathered around as he plumped the heavy gray container at my side. I looked at the scratches around the lock. "No patience I see. You've been at the lock."

"Not me," he said. "That was James. The burns along the seam are where I worked on it."

"And you didn't succeed either. Not only are the contents of this container the latest invention of the great Professor Coypu and the Special Corps laboratory, but the container itself is unenterable, the lock unbreakable. But after I show it my thumbprint here, punch in the correct number . . ."

The top of the container slipped aside and they all leaned forward as I reached in and extracted a black metal box. It had a hole in the top and a switch on its side and I held it up for examination.

"Not too impressive," Angelina sniffed.

"All in the eye of the beholder, my love. You will quickly

discover that what it can do is next to miraculous. It is a molecular extractor and restorer, or MES as the acronym builders would have it. When you see it in action you will grow weak with awe." I rooted deep in the container and extracted a tiny object. "James, what would you say that this is?"

He took it in the palm of his hand, turned it around and around as he squinted at it, then handed it back.

"A very detailed model of a heavy mortar."

"Right, but not exactly right. It is a full-sized mortar that has had ninety-nine percent of its molecules removed. All we must do is replace the missing molecules and it will be restored to its original condition."

"Are you sure you don't want to rest?" Angelina asked. "You might even have a fever from that wound."

"Scoff now and repent at leisure!"

I set the MES on the ground, then pulled a cable from its side, which I clipped to the miniature mortar. There was an expanding plastic funnel in the box, which I opened out then plugged into the orifice on top of the machine.

"All that is missing is a source of raw material. Sand, stones, debris of any kind, just dump it into the funnel, boys, and keep it full. That's it; let me know when you are ready. Good—then here we go!"

I reached out and flipped the switch on its side and it began to whine petulantly. Nothing else happened. I saw the skeptical looks.

"Patience," I cozened. "It takes a few moments to strip the molecules down to their component particles—ahh there it goes."

It was like watching a balloon being pumped full of air, although in this case the mortar was being pumped full of steel. As the level of debris fell in the hopper the mortar began to swell, larger and larger, growing and expanding before our eyes as though we were looking at it through a three-dimensional zoom lens. Within a minute it was full-size. A bell pinged and the whine of operation died away.

"Any doubters now?" I asked, reaching out and rapping the barrel. It gave out the ring of pure steel.

"This is really great, Dad," Bolivar said, twirling the range adjustments as James squinted through the sight. "It means we can take any kind of heavy equipment with us by squeezing out all the excess mass. Say . . ."

"I'll bet you've got a number of interesting things already in that box." James finished the sentence for him.

"I do—and we're going to use one right now. Let's just squeeze that mortar down to size first."

I flipped the switch in the opposite direction and the mortar began to shrink as the whine built up. A steady stream of dust poured from an orifice on the MES's side.

"Steel molecules," I said. "Ninety-nine out of every hundred being whipped away."

When the process was completed I put the miniature mortar away and took out a complex machine that rested lightly in the palm of my hand.

"A tissue regenerator and healer, the kind that they have only in the big hospitals. Twenty-four hours in this machine and my arm will be as good as new. I am sure that we all agree I must be in tip-top shape before we start this election campaign."

The boys shoveled the molecular steel back into the hopper and the sturdy medical machine grew before our eyes. When it was life-size again it was but the work of a moment to pull out its power leads and plug them into the atomic generator of the touring car. Angelina carefully removed the bandages from my arm—it really was a mess—and I lay back in the beneficial embrace of the machine. It hummed therapeutically and industriously and I felt better already.

I was almost sorry to leave our bosky dell a day later. The tissues of our spirits, as well as the tissues of my arm, had been restored by our stay here. The weather was perfect, the air clear, the pressures none. Angelina and I talked quietly while she knitted; she was using monomolecular fiber to make a bulletproof vest. The boys paid court to Flavia who basked in the warmth of their attention and forgot for the moment the ordeal that she had been through. But once my arm had healed the old itch for action began to scratch for attention. Angelina knew that the picnic in paradise was over when she saw me oiling up the needle guns.

"Start packing things away, boys," she said. "We'll be leaving soon."

After that it was just a matter of steady driving. Flavia's father had been an agricultural inspector and her early years had been spent traveling with him all over the interior. She knew it well. This enabled her to lead us by mountain tracks, along the escarpment and up through the foothills, staying

away from farms and towns as much as possible. We passed
the occasional smallholding or wood-cutting party, but little
else. When we finally dropped down to the central plateau
we were already within sight of our goal.

"There," she announced, "the terrain of the Marquéz de la
Rosa."

"Where?" I asked, gazing out at the horizon-to-horizon
expanse of copse and field, hill and forest.

"Everywhere. It's all his. Hundreds of thousands of hect-
ares. The nobility are feudal lords on Paraiso-Aqui, the main
reason why Zapilote succeeded in his democratic revolution.
While many of hereditary aristocracy are immensely cruel to
the peasantry, the marquéz is one of the few exceptions.
Which is why it is so important to enlist him on our side."

"Consider that done," I told her. "I'm the last of the
big-time recruiting sergeants. Bolivar, kindly stop here, before
we reach the entrance."

Impressive stone tiers stood before us on both sides of the
road, the pair of them surmounted with an ornate arch deeply
graven with a noble coat of arms. The shield was full of
quarterings, an interesting bar sinister which hinted at lusty
ancestry, plus plenty of griffins, lions and other heraldic
beasts. I dug deep into the refrigerator and took out the ice
bucket. It had a false bottom with even more ice concealed
beneath.

"For you, my jewel," I said to Angelina, slipping a 400-carat
diamond ring onto her finger. She made appreciative gasping
noises which accelerated when I passed over the matching
necklace. "A few items I have been saving for the right
occasion."

"They're gorgeous!"

"Like to like. And a bauble or two for myself to impress
our host." Such as a ring with a ruby the size of a bird's egg,
with matching ruby-studded band for my hat. The twins
clapped appreciatively and Flavia could only stare in shocked
silence. I hoped the marquéz would be as impressed as well.

"Onward to meet our destiny!" I ordered, and we rolled
elegantly through the gates.

The smooth road wound up through green meadows, which
gradually gave way to a series of ornate gardens. A last swoop
through flower-hung trees opened out into a vista of parkland
set with fountains, before a last bend of the road that ended
before the house. Or mansion, castle, whatever. Most impres-

sive, if a little gaudy. Turrets, pillars, mullions, towers, acres of windows and rows of crenellation. An ornately dressed figure appeared through the open front doors, and stood awaiting our arrival with great dignity.

"The marquéz?" I asked, greatly impressed.

"His butler," Flavia said. "Give him your name, and title— if you have one."

Do I have one! A dozen, or more, as many as my fertile imagination can invent. I thought swiftly as James opened the car door, then stalked forth to meet the butler who had descended the stairs to meet me.

"I presume this is the residence of his excellency Gonzales de Torres the Marquéz de la Rosa?"

"It is . . ."

"Good. I was concerned that I had the address right. One castle looks so much like another. Kindly convey to your master the good tidings that the Duke of diGriz is here with his retinue."

"Thank you, thank you. Follow me if you please." As he ushered us inside he whispered to another flunky who hurried away. We paced through cool corridors, sinking deep into the pile of priceless carpets, to a pair of great wooden doors, which he threw open with a grand gesture while announcing me in a stentorian voice. Head high I swept by.

The marquéz came forward, hand extended. A handsome man with just a touch of gray at his noble temples, lithe and strong with an athlete's walk. I took the proferred hand and bowed slightly.

"Welcome, Duke, welcome," he said with some sincerity.

"Jim, if you please, on my world we are most informal."

"Of course, most intelligent. Then you are not of this planet? May I congratulate you on your perfect command of our language. I thought your title was an unfamiliar one."

"Yours however is known across the civilized galaxy. I would not have burst in on you like this had I not been encouraged by one of your relatives who gave me this letter of introduction."

I passed over the note from Jorge, which put the final stamp of approval on our visit. Introductions were made all around, including to the marqueza, who made her appearance, her jewelry not half as impressive as Angelina's I was happy to note. When the others cleared out de Torres, as he insisted I call him, and I settled down with a great flask of excellent wine. I got right to the point.

"I assume that you know that your third cousin four times removed is part of the resistance movement?"

"I didn't know it but it gives me great pleasure to hear that Jorge is working against that monster Zapilote, that degenerate piece of offal that . . ."

He waxed on enthusiastically in this vein for some time and I made mental notes of some of the more fascinating insults.

"I gather from that that you don't exactly see eye to eye with the General-President."

I sipped at the wine until he ran down a second time. I knew that we had a valuable recruit as I nodded unhappy agreement to his words and made my pitch.

"What you say must be true, for tales of this monster's crimes have even reached my home world of Solysombra, many light-years away. What we find most disturbing is that these crimes are committed in the name of democracy, a system we have come to appreciate. I know, sip some wine, that's it, must think about the blood pressure, the two words *are* the same. Like you, people of our class had certain suspicions when the ballot box replaced hereditary rule. But in the long run it worked out all to the good. Particularly when those of noble blood and decent education ran for office themselves. And were elected."

The marquéz lifted one aristocratic eyebrow but was too well-bred to doubt my word aloud.

"It is true, de Torres, if you will think about it. The fact that the aristocracy rules before there are elections does not necessarily mean that it must stop ruling after elections. What it does mean is that the people of character and intelligence have a better chance of being elected than those of no character and pointed heads. I don't know how it is here, but we have some so-called noble gentlemen on my world who aren't fit to clean my pigsty."

He nodded agreement. "We have this problem as well. There are well connected people here whom not only wouldn't I admit to my house, I won't profane the air in this room by speaking their names aloud."

"Then we are of a single mind!" I raised my glass as did he and we downed their contents, and I watched with pleasure as they were refilled. "Therefore I volunteer my experience in politics to aid you and your people. There will be two candidates in the next presidential election—and I shall use my considerable professional knowledge to see that there will be a fair election and that the better man will win."

"Can you do that?"

"Guaranteed."

"Then you are the savior of Paraiso-Aqui."

"Not me. Salvation will be the new president's job."

"And who will that man be?"

"It is obvious. None other than your noble self."

He was stunned by the words and sat for long moments with his head lowered. When he finally raised his eyes to mine they were filled with sorrow.

"That cannot be," he said. "It must be another. I regret that I cannot be president."

12

I was swallowing a mouthful of wine when de Torres spoke
these fateful words. I coughed and choked, then finally pulled
myself together. "You won't be president?" I managed to
finally gasp out. "I don't understand."

"My reasons are simple. I have no experience with planetary rule and would not know where to begin. Nor could I
leave my estates here in the hands of others. I have devoted
my whole life to their development. All of these are sound
reasons, but are secondary to my most important reason.
There is another, far better qualified than I. Though I cannot
deny that I am tempted by the post, and the opportunity to
bring down the despicable Zapilote, I must step down in
favor of one more eminently qualified."

"Do I know this paragon?"

"You do. It is yourself."

Now it was my turn to sit and think—and be tempted. And
it was indeed a temptation! A suitable challenge for a man of
my persuasion. But there were barriers.

"But I am not a citizen of this planet," I protested.

"Does that make a difference?"

"Usually. But . . ."

I foundered and sank on that *but*. As an immense idea
sprang fullblown into my brain. It was all there, complete
and shining, and presented with the compliments of my
subconscious. Which must have been cooking up this masterpiece for some time. But there were details that had to be
checked first.

"May I ask a few questions before I give you my answer?"

"By all means."

"Do you have any rustic relatives, well connected but shy
by nature, stay-at-homes who prefer their own withdrawn
company to those of the outer world?"

"Remarkable!" The marquéz shook his head in wonderment as he refilled our glasses but again. "You have just described my grandnephew, Hector Harapo, in a most exact manner. He is Sir Hector of course, a Knight of the Beeday, a minor order. His small estate borders mine—yet it must be ten years since I saw him last. He does nothing but read scientific books in order to develop new strains of bizcocho berries. The truth is that he is not worldly-wise at all, and were it not for my aid he would have been bankrupt years ago."

"He sounds ideal for our purposes. Of what age is he?"

"Roughly yours. About the same build, though he has an immense black beard."

"The beard will be the easiest part. Now, one more question if I may. Would you agree to be vice-president if Sir Hector ran for president? He would do all the work, but you would add the weight of your authority to his campaign."

"Yes, I would be agreeable to that. But I must warn you, as fine a man as he is, Hector is not presidential material."

"I could argue that—I have seen presidential elections where ancient actors and proven crooks have been elected—but that is not the point now. What we must do, if you agree, is that in the name of common decency we must commit what some might consider to be a crime. But you must judge for yourself. What I would like to do is to pull the wool over the voters' eyes in the slightest manner. It will be as nothing compared to Zapilote's electoral crimes. I think that it is possible to run another man in Hector's place. A man of noble birth, shrewd, experienced, hard, determined . . ."

As I talked his eyes opened wider and wider, his smile grew broader and broader, until he could no longer contain himself and interrupted me with a shout.

"Yourself!"

"None other," I said, humbly.

"It is ideal! I can think of no one better suited."

"But there will be difficulties. We must agree on our political platform before we enter into any alliance. You may not like some of the reforms I intend to carry through if elected."

The marquéz waved aside any possible disagreement with a flip of one noble hand. "Nonsense. All men of honor and standing agree on this sort of thing. I know by your title that we will have no problems."

"I don't think it is going to be *quite* that simple. For

instance, what if I were to advocate splitting up the large estates and giving them to the peasants?"

"I would shoot you on the spot," he said with cold simplicity.

"Lucky that I don't believe in that myself!" Which wasn't quite truthful. But I could see where land reform, all kinds of reform, would be a long and slow process on this planet. We would have to start with basics; the longest journey begins with but a single step, as the shoe salesman said. "No land reform, of course. I just said that to mention some of the political questions that we will be asked if this is an absolutely free election. Now there are one or two little reforms that we will have to consider in order to get the popular vote. They are things that I know we don't like in theory, but we must make a few concessions in order to get people to vote for us."

"For example?" de Torres asked, most suspiciously, memory of those divided estates still in mind.

"Well, for example, we must allow universal suffrage, one man, one vote, and that includes women . . ."

"Women! They can't have the same rights as men!"

"Would you care to say that to my wife?"

"No." He rubbed his jaw, deep in gloomy thought. "Nor my wife either. These are dangerous and revolutionary thoughts, but I suppose we must entertain them."

"If we don't the other side will. In order to win we must support the *habeas corpus,* abolish torture and the secret police, support public health, give free milk to babies and divorces to alienated couples. We must recognize the dignity of man—and woman—and enact laws to protect those rights."

In the end he nodded agreement. "I suppose that you are right. All of my workers enjoy those benefits, so it might be argued that the public at large deserves them too. I can see where this political business can get very complicated."

"You can bet your sweet title it is. So let us get down to work and prepare a party platform."

"Are we having a party on a platform?"

"No. A platform is a statement of the things we intend to accomplish after we have been elected. A party in this context is the political organization that we will form to see that we will be elected."

"That sounds reasonable. And what is the name of our party?"

As he asked the answer sprang fullblown to mind.

"It shall be called the NPWP, the Nobles and Peasants and Workers Party."

"Nip-wip; has a nice ring to it. So let it be."

It was the beginning of a memorable evening. Another bottle of priceless wine was cracked and we sat, heads together like the conspirators that we were, making our detailed plans. The marquéz was no dummy about life on Paraiso-Aqui, and he knew everyone worth knowing as well. He had food sent in when we became hungry and the session continued far into the night. By morning we were thick as thieves, with all the details worked out, and we retired with feelings of virtue at a job well done.

I told Angelina what had been accomplished while we breakfasted in bed in regal style. But de Torres was no slugabed like me. By the time I appeared he already had the wheels well in motion. He had dispatched his estate manager at dawn to take over operation of Sir Hector's estate—and had the befuddled knight returned in the same car. You could only admire energy like this. I could see that de Torres would be quite an asset during the election. I met Hector, who had little idea of what was happening, and just sat stroking his great black beard and muttering to himself. A good beard and easy enough to duplicate from photographs. I hoped he would appreciate what good works I would be doing in his name!

It was then that our first emergency struck. I was actually considering a morning drink, to give me an appetite for lunch, when de Torres came stamping out of his study.

"Something is happening," he said. "An emergency message is on its way. Come with me."

I hurried after him to the elevator, where I had my first look at one of the mechanical artifacts I would soon learn to appreciate. The operator closed the bronze gate behind us, and turned to his valves.

Valves? I must have spoken aloud because de Torres smiled and waved proudly in their direction as the ornate cage of the elevator shuddered slightly, then began to smoothly rise.

"I see you are impressed—nor do I blame you. In the cities you see nothing but shoddy electronics and weak little motors. But in the country we know how to build things better. The forests supply our fuel, the steam plant produces the unleashed energy to pump the water. Hydraulic systems are indestructible. See how smoothly we mount on the piston that supports this cage!"

"A wonder!" I said, and meant it. The cylinder must be buried deep in the foundation, the piston at least a hundred meters long. I hoped their metallurgy was up to it. I watched the water drip slowly from the row of valves and sighed with relief when the gate finally opened.

I had more mechanical joys in store. No simple radio or telephone room awaited us. Instead there was an exhausting climb up a circular staircase to a turret room that stood high above the rest of the castle. A half-dozen men labored here, amidst the hot smell of metal and the hiss of escaping steam. Thick pipes came up through the floor to feed a hulking black engine studded with wheels, levers and gauges. This machine was silent for the moment and all attention was upon the man who stood squinting through a powerful telescope, shouting out numbers.

"Seven . . . two . . . niner . . . four . . . unsure . . . end of line. Send a repeat for that last phrase."

The machine operator began industriously working his handles. The device groaned, hissed and clanked as tall pistons pushed shining steel rods up and down. I followed their movements upwards through the wrought-iron-framed glass roof, and farther up still to the top of the spire where great metal arms jerked and waved.

"I see you are impressed by our semaphore," de Torres said proudly.

"Impressed is far too mild a word," I said truthfully. "How far has this message come?"

"All the way from the coast, relayed from station to station. It is a private enterprise of the larger landowners. We are in constant communication with one another in this manner. The code we use is secret, known to but a handful of us. This message began with a highly urgent signal in clear, which is why I brought you. I feel in my bones that it is concerned with our mutual affairs. Aha, here we are."

The faulty line had been retransmitted and transcribed, the completed message rushed to the marquéz. He frowned down at the rows of numbers, then waved me after him to a chamber built into one wall. A high window threw light onto a carved desk, upon which he spread out the message. From his wallet he took a cipher wheel, set it to a number, then spun the actuator.

"It will go faster," he said, "if you transcribe as I decode."

I wrote out the message as he gave it to me and the knot of

tension in my midriff grew as letter followed letter. When it was finished he leaned over my shoulder and read in silence.

ELECTION LAWS SECRETLY CHANGED
AND PRESIDENTIAL CANDIDATES
MUST REGISTER BY SIX TONIGHT
IN PRIMOROSO—JORGE

"The trouble is already starting," I said. "Zapilote must have got wind of our plans and is moving to stop us before we even get off the ground. What is Primoroso?"

"Our capital city—and Zapilote's stronghold. The man is impossible to beat! If we try to register we will be arrested, and if we don't show up he wins the election by default."

"Never say die before the fight, de Torres. Can we reach Primoroso in time?"

"Easily. My jet copter will take us there in less than three hours."

"How many will it hold?"

"Five, including the pilot."

"The perfect number. You and me, Bolivar and James."

"But your sons are so young. I have armed men—"

"Young in years but wise in experience. You will see for yourself what they can do. Now if you will roll out your craft, I'll get the boys and make a few other arrangements."

I was rooting around in the depths of the storage compartments in the car when Angelina tapped me on the shoulder.

"You are not leaving me behind while you dash off all over the place."

"Indeed I'm not," I said, dropping an armload of equipment and turning to embrace her. "Yours is the most important task since you must stay here and hold our flank. As soon as we are gone you must set up the defenses. As well as firing up the detection apparatus. If we have to come back in a hurry, I look forward to returning to a stoutly defended position. I know nothing of the castle's defenses—but I know a lot about ours, and know that I can rely upon them. And upon you."

She tilted her head most attractively to the side and looked at me quizzically. "You're not inventing all of this on the spot to get me out of the action, are you, diGriz?"

"Never!" I protested mightily, not daring to admit that she had seized instantly upon the truth. "This is going to be a hit-and-run raid, and we will need you in support here. There will be plenty of work for all of us before this rigged election runs to its crooked end. Now please help me find the makeup box. I need a large and black beard for instant use."

She thought hard, then nodded reluctantly. "All right. But you better not be lying to me. If you get burned in this operation I'll kill you for it." Which is a perfect example of female logic that I knew better than to draw to her attention.

Thirty minutes later I was kissing her goodby through the muffling shrouds of the fake beard, and working hard to conceal my pleasure. Good things were going to happen! Round one in the big election campaign was about to begin.

13

We exited together. The twins were dressed in the drab castle livery which served to enhance the marquéz's and my finery. We were impressively eye-catching, a sartorial symphony of feathered hats, bullion waistcoats, sweeping cloaks, and thigh-high boots, everything the peasantry expected a grandee to be. This might give us a chance to score points with the bureaucrats—as well as helping to conceal a choice bit of weaponry.

The copter was shining new and well maintained—no leaking hydraulic pipes here! As proud as de Torres was of the old technology, he was not loath to use shoddy electronics and weak little motors when they suited his needs. In truth, the jet motors of the copter were anything but weak. We hurtled up to cruising altitude and barrelled off towards the eastern coast. The marquéz had a grim look as he planned ahead.

"If we go to the heliport we will have immense difficulties getting past the city walls and on to the Presidio, where the registration must take place."

"What is this Presidio where we have to go?"

"An ancient fort, traditional seat of government of the kings of Paraiso-Aqui. Alas, now occupied by the usurper."

"Can we land there?"

"It is forbidden. But Zapilote goes there by copter all the time, landing in Freedom Square just outside."

"Good enough for him, good enough for us. The worst they can do is give us a parking ticket."

"The worst they can do is shoot us," de Torres said gloomily.

"Cheer up!" I pointed to the small case I was carrying. "In addition to all the documents, there are a few items in here to help us fight back. Nor are the twins completely unarmed."

"No indeed," Bolivar said, swinging about in his seat and patting himself at armpit and hip.

70

"Plenty of heat here," James said, patting as well, as he finished his brother's sentence. "Do we eat before or after the ruckus?"

"Now." I passed over a bag of sandwiches I had extracted from the castle kitchen. "I know your appetites. Don't litter with the wrappings."

"Yes," de Torres said, his mind still on more important things. "We land in the square. They won't be expecting that."

"But will they be expecting us at all?"

"Undoubtedly. They will have us on radar long before we arrive."

"Then let us not make it easy for them. A little misdirection is in order. If we were to land at the heliport how would we get to the Presidio?"

"I would radio ahead for a car and driver to meet us."

"Then do that—right now. The car goes to the heliport, so do the troops—and we land in the square. The pilot takes off as soon as he has set us down and goes on to the heliport where he is supposed to be. The pressure will be off at the heliport by that time. So he can land, then send the car to the Presidio to pick us up when we come out."

He grabbed up the radio controls with alacrity. "An excellent plan, Jim, which I will put into effect this instant."

After that it was just waiting. I dozed in the chair, not so much to demonstrate my nonchalance before battle but rather to catch up on the sleep I had missed the night before. I didn't need a prognostication machine to tell me that it was going to be a busy day.

"Landing in about a minute, Dad. Thought you would like to know."

"And right you are, James," I said, snapping my eyelids open and yawning. I did some muscle stretching and tensing as we floated over the outskirts of a good-sized city and down towards the white strip of a heliport. Just beyond it was an ancient city wall, penetrated now by modern roads. It all looked quiet. Perhaps too quiet.

"Full power—*now*!" de Torres called out, and the pilot kicked in the throttle.

We arched up over the wall, skidded across the rooftops and whipped about in a sharp turn around a great and gloomy fortress. Obviously our target. The few pedestrians in Freedom Square fled in panic from the downblast of our jets. We hit and bounced and my boys bailed out, one to each side. They helped the old folks down, slammed the doors—and the copter was up and away almost before the locals knew we had arrived. Then, with the marquéz leading the parade, we quick-marched across the square towards the entrance to the Presidio.

Our first problem was so slight that we scarcely noticed it. A beribboned junior officer popped out from between the gates and barred our way.

"It is illegal to land in the square. Do you realize . . ."

"I realize I want you out of my way, little man," de Torres said in the coldest of tones, hundreds of generations of noble lineage vibrating from every word. The officer gasped and paled and practically wilted aside. We marched on. Up the steps and into the entrance hall. The official behind the desk there leapt to his feet at our approach.

"Where is the registration for the presidency election taking place?" de Torres demanded.

"I do not know, excellency," the man gasped.

"Then find out," de Torres said, picking the man's phone off the desk and handing it to him. He had no choice other than to obey. Beneath the blaze of the marquéz's gaze he even managed to get the right answer.

"The third floor, excellency. The lift is there . . ."

"The stairs are here," I broke in, pointing the way. "There could be an accident, the power cut perhaps."

"Perhaps." The marquéz nodded agreement and off we stamped.

We had actually penetrated to the right office and obtained the correct registration forms before the opposition arrived in strength. I was already scratching away at the forms when the door crashed open and a crowd of nasties pushed in. They wore black uniforms, black caps and black glasses. Their fat fingers were close to the butts of their long black pistols. I had no doubt at all that I had finally met the dreaded Ultimados, the dictator's personal murder squad. They opened their ranks and a potbellied officer in full dress uniform pushed his way through. His wrinkled face was livid with rage, his ancient, yellowed fingers scratched at his holstered pistol. The opposition had arrived.

"Cease what you are doing at once!" he ordered.

The marquéz turned slowly towards him, cold lips at full

sneer. "Who are you?" he asked with an insulting mixture of boredom and superiority.

"You know who I am, de Torres," Zapilote screeched, the frog mouth drawn into an angry line. "What is that bearded moron attempting to do?"

"That gentleman is my grandnephew Sir Hector Harapo, Knight of the Beeday, and he is filling out the application form as a candidate for the presidency of this republic. Is there any reason that he shouldn't?"

General-President Julio Zapilote had not ruled this planet for all the years by accident. I watched as he opened his mouth—then closed it again and took control of his temper. The color faded from his cheeks to be replaced by a far more dangerous icy calculation.

"Every reason," he said, his control matching that of de Torres. "Registration does not open until tomorrow. He can return then."

"Really?" There was no warmth in de Torres's smile. "You should pay closer attention to the operation of the congress. They amended the law this morning so that registration not only opened today—but closed today as well. Would you like to see a copy of the legislation?" He moved his hand towards his breast pocket. Pure bluff and masterfully done. Zapilote shook his head sharply.

"Who would doubt the word of a man of your rank? But Sir Hector cannot register without a birth record, doctor's certificate, voting registration . . ."

"All in here," I said, holding up the case and smiling.

I could almost see the thoughts being ordered in that evil brain. The silence lengthened. His first legal plan was now in ruins since the registration was being made. That left violence as his only remaining option. By the look in that serpentine eye I could see that he was actively considering it. If he could have eliminated us all instantly on the spot, without there being any public knowledge of the deed, I am sure he would have done it. But there had been too many witnesses to our arrival; the marquéz was too public a figure for him to get away with that. Only the nobodies vanish in secrecy in a police state. The silence stretched and stretched—and then he waved his hand in dismissal.

"Complete the application," he ordered me, then turned to de Torres. "And what is your interest in this matter, Gonzales?

Does your grandnephew need his hand held and his nose wiped?"

The marquéz made no mention of the obvious insult of the use of his first name. His calm matched that of the dictator's. "Neither hand-holding nor nose-wiping, Julito." He used the diminutive as a deliberate slap in the face to Zapilote. "I come as his partner. I am standing for the office of vice-president. In due course both of us will be elected, after which we will see to it that your filthy administration is brought low at last."

"No man talks to me like that!" The artificial calm was gone, and Zapilote was quavering with rage, his fingers clutching tightly onto his gun butt.

"I talk to you like that because I am here to see to your destruction, little man."

The marquéz was as angry as Zapilote now, despite the calmness of his tones. Neither of them was going to back down, that was obvious. Death and destruction were in the air.

"Perhaps you can aid me with this application," I said, stepping between them and waving the sheets of paper before Zapilote's face. "Since you are President you should know . . ."

"Step aside, fool," he screeched, pushing at my arm which, however, didn't push too well. We swayed and stumbled and the papers flew up into the air. Raging, he struck me with his fist—full in the face.

With no effect, of course. I rocked with the feeble blow, and was obviously unharmed by it. I looked down at him in bewilderment, then shrugged and bent to pick up the papers.

"Well if you don't know I'll just have to ask someone else," I said as I shambled off.

This bit of nonsense had cleared the air. Zapilote had been distracted, while de Torres had the intelligence to realize what I had done. He turned his back and returned with me to the counter.

"I shall not forget that, Jim," he said, so quietly that only I could hear. "You have saved me from myself." Then aloud. "Let me aid you, Sir Hector, these government forms can be tortuous."

Zapilote might very well have shot us in the back. But I counted upon my sons to handle that possibility if it should arise. He didn't try. Instead there was a mutter of orders being issued and I looked around to see that the confrontation was over and that he was leaving. As the door closed behind the last of his Ultimados I let out the breath that I had not realized I was holding.

"You are right," de Torres said. "Politics can be fascinating. Now let us complete these boring forms and leave."

There were no more interruptions. We scratched away at the applications until they were done, had them stamped and endorsed and took our copies for safekeeping. The first step had been completed. We walked slowly away and back down the stairs with the boys strolling behind as rearguards.

"This is just the beginning," de Torres said. "We now have a murderous enemy who wants us dead as well as defeated."

"Correct. And my feelings are that he is going to do something desperate, and soon. He'll never have us in this exposed a position again."

"He wouldn't dare!"

"He would indeed, Marquéz. You're not on your home ground now. It would be extremely easy to kill us before we leave the city. An angry mob might be to blame, or an assassin who would be killed afterwards. Zapilote would then make all the sympathetic noises and we would be out of the way forever. I guarantee that the story will be a good one."

"Then what should we do?"

"Exactly what we planned. Take the car to the heliport. This little mob will not be as easy to take out as all that. But let's move fast, give him as little time to plan as is possible."

I didn't bother to tell de Torres that our transportation was the next worry. I was relieved to see that a large and luxurious limousine was waiting at the entrance. But just because it was there did not mean Zapilote was not one jump ahead of us. The driver saluted and opened the rear door.

"Bolivar," I said. "Take that man aside and give him a large sum of money. You will drive."

As the bewildered driver was led away by a strong grip on his elbow, I took a small device from my bag and handed it to James. "Run it around the car, will you. It can sniff out any kind of explosives, no matter how well sealed they are."

He slithered under the vehicle like a snake, emerging at the far end a few moments later. "Clean as a whistle," he reported. "Let's see what's under the hood." He ran it along the join in the metal—then stopped. Frozen. He bent over and looked at the fastenings, then slowly opened them. A few seconds later he emerged and stood up with a plastic container in his hand.

"Clumsy," he said. "Wired to the brake pedal. First time the brakes are applied—whammo. But there were no attempts to disguise it, nor is it fitted with booby traps or any other kind of security device."

"They were in a hurry. They won't make that mistake a second time. Let's go."

"Wow," Bolivar said from the driving seat as he engaged the throttle. "This thing runs by steam. I'll need directions. Are we still going to the heliport?"

"Unless there is another way out of town," I said. The marquéz shook his head.

"We are not safe for a moment here. All roads will be blocked and we can count on no one in the city for help."

"To the copter then. By the shortest route if you don't mind."

The marquéz shouted directions and Bolivar drove like a demon. Pedestrians scattered before us as we barreled straight down the middle of the road. We screeched tires around a final turn and there was the city wall ahead. There was a barrier blocking the gate, armed guards with ready weapons stationed at each side of it.

"We've no time for conversation," I said. "Bolivar, slow as though you were going to stop. James and I will use the sleeping gas bombs." I dug a handful from my bag. "No time for the noseplugs—so just hold your breath. When the bombs go—we go! Get ready."

The car slowed before the barrier, then shot forward as the gas bombs exploded into dense clouds of smoke. There was a crunch and a bang and bits of the barrier flew in all directions. Then we were through and picking up speed. If any shots were fired we didn't know it. A screaming two-wheel turn took us around the corner and there was the heliport directly ahead. And our copter.

Which was on fire, with the dead pilot hanging out of the door.

14

"They should not have done that," de Torres said with savage fury. "Killed an innocent man. Not that."

I could understand his feelings—but had little time to consider them. One escape route was closed. I had to find another. Quickly.

"Keep moving!" I called to Bolivar as a car full of troops hurtled around the corner behind us. Could we get another copter? It didn't look like it, the only ones in sight were tethered and silent. The soldiers would be on top of us long before we got airborne.

"What's ahead of us, beyond the heliport?"

"Homes, factories, the suburbs," de Torres said. "After that the highway north. They will cut that off; we will never be able to pass them."

"Perhaps. Straight on, driver!" Spoken in tones of assurance to bolster the troops' morale. But mine was pretty low. We were out of one trap and driving straight into another. Into a nest of local roads with only one exit. Our present freedom was an illusion. They would be closing in on all sides, blocking all exits. There was no escape. At that very instant, an amplified voice spoke these very words aloud.

"There is no escape!"

The voice crashed down upon us like the wrath of the gods. The street behind us was empty for the moment, and nothing visible ahead except the quiet suburban homes. What was it? Bolivar spun the heavy car in its own length and shot it up a side street, driving flat out to escape the mysterious voice.

"You cannot escape. Stop at once or we will fire down upon you!"

Down? I poked my head out of the window and there, just above us, hovered a two-place police floater. It drifted, light as butterfly, held aloft by a gravity generator, the same kind that powered grav-chutes. A nasty-looking, large-orificed

77

weapon pointed straight at me. I pulled my head back in just in time to grab de Torres's wrist. He had extracted a deadly-looking machine pistol from the folds of his cloak and was about to fire.

"Release me! I'll blow those swine out of the air!"

"Don't! I have a better plan. Bolivar, stop the car."

I managed to wrestle the marquéz's gun away from him. Aside from the fact that I am reluctant to kill anyone, even Zapilote's creatures, I really did have a plan.

"Slow down, then stop. We are all going to get out of the car and wave our empty hands in the air. If they wanted to shoot they would have done so already. I'm sure that they have something even more nasty in mind . . ."

The marquéz gasped. "You mean to surrender to these offal—without a fight!"

"Not at all," I reassured him. "We just won't use weapons. I want that floater intact—because that is our ticket out of here. Now—let's move it before any ground support arrives."

The floater just hovered there above our heads as we climbed out, the gun still aimed. I tried not to look at it and sincerely hoped that my theory was correct. Or we were dead.

"*Move away from the car,*" the amplified voice ordered, and we did so. Only then did it slowly settle to the ground.

The pilot wore the green uniform of the police. The man seated beside him, with the large-caliber gun, was all in black, his eyes concealed by black glasses. He waggled the gun in our direction.

"Just keep doing what you are doing now," he said. "I don't want to shoot you, believe me." Then he laughed. "Because that is not what we have in mind. No bullet holes. You're all going to burn to death when your defective copter crashes on takeoff. Isn't that nice? But be warned, I'll shoot if I have to. You're not walking away from this one . . ."

"I can't bear it! My heart . . ." James gasped, clutching his chest, then collapsing to the ground.

"He has a coronary obfuscation!" Bolivar wailed. "I must give him his medicine!" He bent over his brother's limp body.

"Stay away—don't touch him!" the Ultimado ordered, waving his gun at them.

His attention was off de Torres for the moment, who noticed this and spoiled what should have been a smoothly operational plan. The marquéz roared in anger and dived for the secret policeman.

He had too far to go. The machine-gun blasted and de Torres spun about and fell—even as Bolivar moved aside so James could fire. James had drawn his needle gun the instant his brother had come between him and the Ultimado. It spat a cloud of needles that dropped the gunman, then it elevated to send more needles through the open door of the floater, knocking out the pilot before he could aim his own gun.

It was over in an instant. I jumped to the marquéz's side, tore aside the folds of his cloak.

"Damn! Bolivar—quick—the medkit from the floater."

There was blood everywhere. I used my dagger to cut away his sodden clothing. A hole in his leg, not important, a puncture wound in his abdomen. A bad one. Not much that first aid could do here. I sprayed on antibiotic, slapped pressure bandages on the wounds. Turned him a bit and did the same thing to an exit wound in his side. And tried to remember my anatomy. He had been shot in the gut, that was all too obvious, but at first look no important organs seemed to be hit. And the telltale revealed that his vital signs were still good. What was the next step?

"Bolivar—can you fly this thing?"

"I can fly anything, Dad."

"Right. Drag out the pilot and take his place. James, take the marquéz's legs. Gentle does it, up into the seat."

"Shall I get him to a hospital?" Bolivar asked.

"No, that would just be murdering him. The Ultimados would see to it that he never left the place alive. The only chance he has is to get back to the castle. In behind them, James. These two-seaters will carry three in an emergency . . ."

"But, Dad, you . . ."

"They'll never lift four. Start a saline drip going, watch his vital signs, you know what to do—now move. And don't worry about your old dad. He's been in tight spots before. *Lift it!*"

They did. They were good lads. As the floater shot up into the air I dragged the pilot across the road and heaved him into the car. The Ultimado followed; I wasn't quite as gentle with him. Someone looked out of a nearby house, then darted back inside. I had to get out of this area quickly—an important first step for any survival plan I might come up with. I could hear the sirens coming this way already.

As I jumped behind the wheel I realized I should have asked Bolivar for a driving lesson. I didn't share his enthusiasm for antique machinery. All I could do was gape at the hundreds of polished valves, handles, buttons and gauges. But this was no time to gape! I grabbed the largest handle and pulled.

There was a hideous roar, and an immense black and white cloud enveloped the car; I quickly pushed the handle back. I had blown the stack, used live steam to blast clean the exhaust. I worked more gingerly after that. Not too much later, after I had cleaned the windshield, turned on the lights, radio and music player, I succeeded in feeding steam to the engine and we trundled off down the road.

I took the first turning at random, then the next. The road led gradually up into the foothills and the houses began thinning out. I couldn't hear the sirens any more so I slowed in order to attract less attention. But where could I go? There was no escape from airborne observation. They would be on to me any minute now. Another bend revealed a large home with attached garage. A car had just backed out of the garage and had turned into the road.

I hit the brakes, twisted the wheel, bounced over the curb and across the lawn and skidded into the just-vacated garage. I was still braking as the car slammed into the rear wall with metallic bang.

The steering wheel had caught me on the forehead, so I felt very rubber-legged as I climbed down and staggered out into the fresh air. I really wasn't prepared for any conversation with the large and irate man who stood before me.

"Are you insane? What do you mean driving into my garage like this, wrecking it?"

"Urggle," I said, or something that sounded very much like that. I waggled my jaw a bit to free it up.

"What games are you playing at?" Words failed him as he spluttered with rage; violence overcame him. He swung a hard fist at my jaw.

Well, dizzy or no, this was a language I could easily understand. I stepped inside the clumsy blow and let him have a far better aimed, and possibly harder, fist into the midriff. His only option was to fold over and collapse, which he promptly did. A siren shrieked loudly as I stepped over him and clutched the handle of the overhead door. As I pulled it shut I had a quick glimpse of a police cruiser hurtling by. I swallowed loudly and listened for the squeal of the brakes as it stopped, turned, came back . . .

The sound lessened and died away. They hadn't seen me.

For the first time in a century and half I let myself relax. And looked at my watch. That was exaggerating the time span a little bit. In fact less than two hours had passed since we had walked through the front door of the Presidio. So much for subjective and objective time.

Action over for the moment. A question presented itself that needed answering soonest. Was the owner of this garage and house alone? A small window set into the garage door let in a measure of light. I squinted through it to see the owner's car still standing patiently before the house. Empty. All I could do was leave it there for the moment. If there were anyone in the house who saw it and came to investigate, why that bridge would be crossed if it were ever there to cross.

Next step. Plan. The house and car owner stirred and moaned and I gave him surcease from sorrow with a quick needle from my gun. I pondered his now-still form and bits of a plan began to come together. A change of identity was needed since my garish aristocratic rig would easily be noticed. A uniform? A possibility, but eventually a liability. But what about an excellently cut white summer suit, with wide-brimmed matching white hat decorated with a snakeskin band? A very nice one lay on the floor before me; all it needed was dusting off. And the owner of the suit had a car waiting for him outside. Nor did I feel too sorry for this not-too-innocent victim. Anyone who had prospered to his degree under the corrupt Zapilote regime had to be into something not too nice. I rationalized as I stripped him. Trying not to notice that all of his undergarments were lace-edged gold lamé set with scarlet hearts. This hinted at situations best left unconsidered.

The first thing that had to go was my beard. There was solvent in my bag which loosened the adhesive so that I could tear the hair away in big chunks. I stuffed it into the bag to take with me, since the longer the forces of evil thought it was still attached to my face the happier I would be.

The suit made a really good fit as did, surprisingly, his shoes. We were like twins, except of course for our tastes in underwear. And I was still undisturbed. I placed my benefactor tenderly on the rear seat of the car, his feet resting on the face-down form of the unconscious Ultimado thug, then picked up my bag and let myself out of the garage. The sun shone warmly even though it was close to the horizon, there was no sign of activity in the adjoining house—and my car awaited at the curb. As I strolled towards it a large, black police vehicle roared back the way it had come. Paying me no heed at all. My car was bright red and sporty and, how considerate!, the motor had been left running. The controls were far simpler than those of the steam car, so much so that within a minute I was rolling majestically down the street.

Where to? The answer to that one was obvious. Back into the city. By now there would be roadblocks on all the exits from Primoroso. And once the police begin to stop people to ask for identification they always get carried away by enthusiasm. Everyone gets stopped, all the vehicles are searched. And, though we were of the same build, the car-owner's ID would certainly not fit me. No, the best idea was to move away from the action, to seek the security of the big city. Then I could stop and think about the next step. A rat is always safest in the warrens of the city, a stainless steel rat no less.

I worked away at the controls and, after only a few mistakes, folding top up and down, a blast on the horn, I managed to find the music player controls. After this I rolled in comfort back to Primoroso, whistling melodically along with a catchy tune that was all syncopation and percussion.

15

How many hours of freedom did I have left? The answer came back far too quickly. Not many. When it was discovered that both our escape car and the police floater had vanished, the search would surely be intensified. I knew that I had been seen leaving the scene of the action. As soon as this was discovered the search would spiral out from that spot in wider and wider circles. Questions would be asked, houses searched. Garages opened. The car and unconscious men would be found. Then they would know I was driving this car . . . I added another little increment to my speed. The city walls were just ahead, with the traffic still flowing smoothly through them. I flowed as well, saw the bulk of the Presidio up ahead and turned away from it in the opposite direction. I found myself entering a most attractive district, with tall trees along the road and discreet little shops tucked behind striped awnings. And bars, with tables set out on the pavement where people sipped at colorful drinks. Where, undoubtedly, food was served.

As this thought crossed my mind news of it instantly zipped out through my neural network to the rest of my body. Saliva spurted in my dry mouth and my stomach began grumbling like an active volcano. Not a bite had passed my lips since breakfast! That would have to change. The most obvious next step would be to comfort body and soul with drink and food while I planned the immediate future.

The trees vanished, the street narrowed, the snobbish bars gave way to sleazy joints. Depressed-looking men held up the walls of buildings with slumped shoulders and I chortled with joy.

"Perfect, Jim, just perfect. Opportunity knocks and must be admitted at once."

I turned at the next corner and stopped. The neighborhood was ideal for my needs. When I emerged from the car I was so forgetful as to leave the window open, the door unlocked—even the keys dangling beckoningly from the controls. If this machine was not nicked and gone within minutes I would be very surprised. With my trail thus covered for the moment I strolled back towards the bright lights that were just beginning to glow in the dusk.

I'll say this much for Paraiso-Aqui, it has a cuisine that should be known throughout the galaxy. A bottle of chilled wine washed down course after course in an unassuming but absolutely incredible dining establishment. First a tangy soup with albondigas, little meatballs, floating and bobbing in it. This was followed by empanadas, meat-stuffed pastry, a blended green salad mixture called guacamole, then more and more. The restaurant was called The Stuffed Pig and I felt like one myself before I was through. The food was so good that I completely forgot about my predicament until I reached the coffee-brandy-cigar stage. Sighing and puffing I finally managed to force my thoughts back to survival rather than gluttony. I did not care! I could not have profaned that meal by paying attention to anything else. But the food was finished—and if I didn't do something soon I would be as well. I sighed and called for the counting.

I had to take it as proven that by this time our escape car, well stuffed with sleeping uglies, had been found. Which meant that my description was now being broadcast in great detail. Happily, at least half of the male population of this part of the city were dressed as I was. And they would still be looking for the man with the black beard. All of these factors would slow things down—but not stop them. I paid, over-tipping lavishly, and was ushered by servile waiters back to the reality of harsh existence.

And I really had been thinking ahead. This entire world went to sleep in the midday heat, after gorging themselves comatose on food and drink. They did not wake again until the sun was low. Which meant that the shops would still be open and I could get the items that I would need.

One item at a time. A new hat here, a jacket there, a shirt in a different store. When I had what I needed I stopped for a cool drink as a reward for my labors. Does it come as a surprise that after a visit to the washroom of the establishment a different individual emerged? It does not. The old garments vanished in a dark alley and the only task remaining was to make my way to safety.

Yes, that was all. Alone in the dark and alien city, the euphoria of the day worn off, fatigue settling in, my face badly in need of shaving, my morale at a new low, I sought escape in a dimly lit bar. All men's hands were turned against me.

"You look lonely, handsome stranger."

But not all women's! She was sultry and brash, her charms abundantly obvious in the low-cut dress. Solace and a hiding place for the night?

I shook my head *no* and she cruised away. Not only would Angelina skin me and rub salt into my flayed flesh if she had even a wisp of suspicion of a liaison of this kind but—more realistically—these girls were watched by the police and their pimps were all informers. I had to come up with a far better plan.

While I was trying to think of one it was handed to me on a silver platter. The two men who stood beside me at the bar were talking together, loud enough to be overheard.

". . . never showed up, did he?"

"No. I guess something else came up."

"Lets us down, doesn't it? Poker is no good with a player short."

I turned slowly, smiled broadly—and hesitantly tapped the nearest man on the arm.

"Excuse me, I couldn't help overhearing. I'm a stranger in town. All alone. And I do love a game of cards with friends. I don't play very well but, gee, like they say, it's just a friendly game."

The man turned slowly towards me, and if his grin was very much like that of a crocodile who was I to care. "Why that's great. We're just passing through town ourselves. Just like you, we enjoy a friendly game, a little fun. Why don't you join us?"

This pair were so obviously sharpers that they should have worn placards around their necks. And they wanted to con a con man! It's not every day that you can get blessed like this. And the last thing they wanted was interference from the police. I was led, a lamb for the slaughter, from the bar to a cab and then to their hotel room, where a sultry and most attractive woman admitted us. The evening promised to be a highly entertaining one!

"Sit down, have a drink," one of my hosts said, the smaller

of the two. "I'm Adolfo, and this big guy is Santos, and my girl friend here is Renata, and I didn't catch your name?"

"Jaime."

"That's great, Jaime. How about a glass of ron before we start."

"Never said no yet."

I was beaming with pleasure, enjoying every minute of this. Renata mixed and served the drinks while Adolfo cracked out some decks of cards and the chips. Santos was big and burly and looked slow but I knew he was not. He was the heavy who took care of any trouble. Adolfo hummed to himself as he opened the first deck of cards and shuffled them, said *oops* and smiled when he fumbled and the cards splattered onto the table. Ha! I imagine he could shuffle and palm almost as well as I could.

"Cut for deal?" he asked, and we did. My king was highest and I took the pack. "Dealer's choice OK?" To which they nodded enthusiastically. "Three card draw then, for starters." I shuffled, Santos cut, and the fun began.

The play went smoothly and Renata kept our glasses filled. When she wasn't performing this important function she sat by the window, with the radio turned low, listening to music. While I was delicately led down the garden path. Nothing obvious at first. The play ran fairly except for the fact that when he shuffled Adolfo worked some large cards to the bottom and saw to it that I was dealt these from time to time. This gave me a mild winning streak. I chortled as I raked in the chips.

"Sorry to take your money boys."

"That's how the cards fall," Adolfo said magnanimously. He dealt and the cards flicked into place.

"What do you think of the election?" I asked, picking up my cards and fanning them out. Two pair, tens full on sixes. "You've got to be joking," Adolfo said. "Cards?"

"One. No, I mean it. I heard that an independent was running against Zapilote." I discarded and drew another ten. I opened my eyes slightly and raised the bet as well. Adolfo matched me and raised. Santos folded. Renata brought me a new drink.

"No way, and I mean no way," Adolfo said. "Anyone runs against The Buzzard is subject to sudden heart attacks. What do you have?"

"Full house."

"So do I. Jacks high. About time I won something. I was afraid you were going to skin us, you and your winning streak."

Me and my losing streak. The cards began to go against me and very soon all of the money in my wallet was gone.

"That's it for me, boys," I said, folding my last hand. "I'm skinned. Unless I dig into my traveling money."

"Up to you, Jaime," Adolfo said casually. "Just a friendly game. But you should have a chance to win something back."

"You're right, what the dickens. Just a friendly game."

I went over to my case, where I had placed it on the table in plain sight, and opened it. As I reached into it Santos called out to me, his voice suddenly quite rough.

"Just hold it there, Jaime. Don't take anything out of that case sudden-like if you don't mind."

I looked up and saw that he had a large pistol in his hand, which he was leveling at me. And little Adolfo was doing the same thing with another gun. Just to make the scene complete, Renata had produced an equally impressive pistol from someplace, which was also pointed in my direction. I smiled, innocently I hoped, and moved my hands slowly into sight.

"Say, what's going on here?" I asked.

Santos's only answer was to cock his pistol with a snik-click, the tiny sound loud in the silence of the room.

16

"What happened to our friendly poker game?" I said.

"What happened to our friendly traveler who just wanted to play poker?" Adolfo asked.

"What are you talking about?"

"I'm talking about the fact that we have an X-ray screen tucked up under that table top. You have exactly ten seconds to tell us why you have three guns in there. Mr. Police Spy."

I laughed at this suggestion, then stopped laughing when Adolfo cocked his gun too. "Only a police spy would talk politics to a stranger," he said grimly. "Seven seconds."

"Stop with the counting!" I said. "All right. I'll tell you the truth. I'm a card sharper. I was just about to clean you out."

"What?" Adolfo shook his head as though to clear it. This was undoubtedly the last answer he had been expecting.

"You don't believe me? I've been watching you all evening while you marked the edges of the high cards with your thumbnail. So you could separate them out of the pack, then deal from the bottom. I let you lift my bundle so I could go into my reserves, bet high, lose, double or nothing—then clean you out with one last hand. The guns are to make sure I get out of here with the winnings."

"You're lying to save your neck," Adolfo said, but he didn't sound as assured now. "No one could do that to me."

"No? I will be happy to demonstrate. You just shuffled the deck that's on the table didn't you?" He nodded. "All right then, I'm going over to the table and pick it up. I won't make any fast moves so try to keep those fingers cool on the triggers."

I did just that. Moving slowly, sitting down, pulling my chair forward, reaching out and picking up the deck right under their noses. They stared intently while I dealt out three hands. I sat back and clasped my hands behind my neck, the picture of relaxation, and nodded my chin down at my cards.

"There they are, Adolfo, my old card mechanic. You pick up my cards and see what kind of a hand mother luck has dealt me."

His gun was lowered, forgotten, as he reached out and turned my hand over.

Four aces and a joker stared back at him.

"Five aces usually win," I said calmly, smiling, as both men stared down at the cards. Renata leaned over so she could see too.

I shot her first, then Santos. With the needle gun I had thoughtfully tucked into the back of my collar. Adolfo jumped with surprise as his companions slumped and banged towards the floor. He started to raise his gun again but mine was already leveled right between his eyes.

"Don't try it," I growled, just as grimly as I could. "Lay it down and you won't get hurt. Don't worry about your partners, they're just asleep."

He was trembling as he put the gun down. I grabbed it up along with Santos's, then threw them both onto the couch. Renata's gun was on the carpet by her limp hand and I kicked that one away as well. Only then did I relax, put my own gun away, and take a long swig from my glass.

"Do you always X-ray your marks' luggage?" I asked.

He nodded, still shocked by the rapidity of events, then finally got the words out. "If we can. See if they're carrying heat, anything. Renata does it after the game starts, then signals us what's in the bag."

"A good code. I never noticed it. Listen, if I bring your friends around do you promise no more strongarm stuff? And you can keep the money you won as a sign of good faith."

"You mean that? Who are you? Police . . .?"

I decided to take a chance on a measure of frankness.

"You have it the wrong way around. The main reason I jumped at a chance of a game tonight was because every policeman in town was looking for me. I didn't think they would look here."

He whinnied and shied away. "You're the guy on the radio! The mass murderer who killed forty-two people . . ."

"No. I'm the guy on the radio all right, but the mass murderer is their cover story. I'm the guy who is working for the opposition to try and get Zapilote kicked out of office."

"You mean that?" He was excited now, his fear gone. "If you are going to take The Buzzard out, why I'm on your side. They got the rackets so sewn up that it's hard for a grifter to make an honest living."

"One of the best reasons I have ever heard for clean government!" I extended my hand. "Put it there, Adolfo. You have just joined the political party. I can guarantee that when our man is elected that the dumbest cop on the planet will be put in charge of the bunco squad."

We shook enthusiastically on that. Then I dug out the pressure spray hypo of antidote and gave his snoring associates a shot each, but only after I had taken the precaution of locking their guns safely away in my case.

"They'll come around in about five minutes," I said, as we propped them comfortably on the couch.

"I have a question," he said. "I admit you got me. I *know* I shuffled that deck right. So how did you deal yourself that hand?"

"I did what you weren't expecting," I told him, not able to keep all the pride from my voice. What joy to beat a pro at his own game! "Look at the deck."

He did, fanning the cards in a swift arc across the table. One glimpse did it. "The aces are still here—and the joker . . ." He gaped up at me and burst out laughing. "Palmed from the old deck."

"Exactly, I slipped them out when we discarded it. You were so busy stacking this deck that you never noticed."

"You're really good, Jaime." Ahh, what wonderful words! "Your hands were empty when you sat down at the table. Of course—you reached down to pull your chair close. Palmed the extra cards then. Slipped them on the bottom of the deck. Dealt your own hand from the bottom and that was that."

We kept the conversation at this professional level for quite awhile. I showed him a holdout and a pass that had never reached this planet, in exchange for a very nifty substitution. By the time Santos stirred and groaned to life we were thick as thieves. The big man muttered, licked his lips, opened his eyes—and roared with anger as he hurled himself at me. Adolfo put out his foot and tripped him so he sprawled out at our feet.

"He's a friend," Adolfo said. "Let me explain."

Since the little man was the brains of the outfit they

accepted me at once. To seal the bond of friendship I opened
my bag and gave each of them a crisp packet of money.

"To close the contract," I said. "You're on the party payroll
now. With my personal guarantee that you will be in on the
payoff at the end. The new president will do exactly what I
tell him to." Which was the absolute truth considering the
fact that *I* was going to be that president. "The first thing you
can do is help me get back in contact with my people. Do you
ever work the tourists in Puerto Azul?"

"That's like suicide!" Adolfo gasped, while the others nodded horrified agreement. "The only off-planet currency we
ever get on this planet comes from them. The Ultimados
would butcher us in a second if we went near the tourists.
We keep our heads down, work a few country marks that
come to the big city, give a cut to the police for protection.
They make sure that the Ultimados don't know we exist."

"Could you go to Puerto Azul?"

"No reason why not. Our travel papers are in order."

"That's good enough. I have a contact there who can get a
message through to the Marquéz de la Rosa, who will see to
it that I get help."

"Do you know him?" Renata asked in a hushed voice. Even
crooks are impressed by the aristocracy.

"Know him? We had breakfast together this morning. The
only question now is—what will the message be?" And even
more important—and depressing thought—what if the marquéz
were no longer alive? Had they made it back to the castle all
right—or had they been intercepted on the way? Were Bolivar and James all right? Or had they been . . . ?

I paced the floor, unthinking, obsessed with worry now
that I was out of trouble myself. I could plan nothing until I
found out what the situation was. But how could I contact the
castle?

Ask the right question and you get the right answer.
"Adolfo," I wheeled about and stabbed a finger in his direction. "You know what happens around here. Have you ever
heard of the semaphore system that the aristocrats use?"

"Who doesn't know? Every time you pass one of the castles
there are the arms waving and flapping. Those people live in
the dark ages. Why don't they put in telephones . . ."

"What do you mean every time you pass a castle? Aren't
they on the other side of the barrier?"

"No such way. There's one down the road not two Ks from here."

"Then we are in business? Any trouble getting inside?"

"No trouble, but you have to pass two policemen at the gate. Show identification and that kind of thing."

"That's no good for me. But if I could get a message inside." I looked at Renata. "Are your papers all right?" She nodded. "They better be. We pay the police enough for them."

"Then you can carry the message. Now describe the physical setup of the castle's entrance so I can work out a plan for getting me inside." I dug more money from my bag, I was very free with the marquéz's funds, and passed it over. "This should cover expenses. Now—speak!"

I kept the plan simple, like all good plans should be, nevertheless it was past dawn before I had worked the details out. Another sleepless night; this was getting to be a habit. Adolfo was playing solitaire, Santos was asleep on the couch, and I assumed that Renata was doing the same in the bedroom. "Adolfo," I said. "What time do the shops open in this fine city?" He looked at his watch.

"In about two hours."

"Just the time we need to enjoy our breakfasts and go over the details of the exercise. I'll call room service while you sound reveille."

Two pots of coffee replaced the night's sleep. I sipped at the last cup and finished the preparations for the coming operation. In the castle, while I had been transcribing the message for the marquéz, I had managed to liberate some of his stationery. By reflex, really. I scarcely realized at the time that I had been doing it. But letterheads would be very useful right now. I wrote the note on one of them, forged the marquéz's signature with an exactitude that brought a murmur of praise from Adolfo, sealed the note into an envelope and passed it over to Renata. "You know what you are to do?" I asked. She nodded.

"No problems. I stop at the milliners and make some purchases. Take a cab. Say I am delivering for the store. The cops let me in. I see that the duke gets the letter. Then I leave and you take over from there."

"Perfect. Stress the urgency of the arrangements to be sure that he gets the timing right. If not I will be very embarrassed. Let's go."

Can you trust crooks, even well-bribed crooks? That was my depressing thought later that morning as zero hour approached. If all went correctly my new allies would be at their positions now, with the final stages of the operation about to begin. I patted my black beard, glued back into position as soon as they had left the hotel room, and looked at the target. The sidewalk cafe was well placed for this job, no further than two hundred meters from the high wall that ringed Castle Penoso. Four steps led up from the pavement to an iron-bound doorway. Two policemen stood at the foot of those steps. I had watched Renata approach and be stopped and questioned by them, then pass through with her bundle. She had emerged without it—which meant the message had been passed. I looked at my watch. Now the moment for the final stage had arrived. I picked up my bag, threw coins on the table, stood, and walked slowly down the street towards the entrance.

The policemen were at the foot of the steps, hands on their guns, looking at the passersby. A extremely well-built young woman slid sinuously by, which drew their attention, as well as low voiced murmurs of approval. Nothing else happened. Where were my troops? Were they late—or not coming? I bent to tie my shoe. I would be noticed if I stayed this close very much longer.

Then, above the normal traffic sounds, I heard the stressed whine of a car's engine, growing louder and louder. I walked slowly on.

I had almost reached the doorway when the screech of brakes sounded. Both policemen looked up as the automobile careened down the road, weaving from side to side—to crash into the curb on the other side of the street. An arm dropped limply from the driver's window.

As the policemen started across the street I bounded up the four steps and pushed hard against the door.

It was locked.

17

There's nothing like a whiff of panic to clear the head. As the adrenalin pumped through my veins, all traces of fatigue vanished on the instant. What was wrong? The door should have been open—they had my message. I pushed again with the same lack of result.

When I looked over my shoulder I saw that the policemen had reached the car. But as soon as they got close the limp arm vanished back inside and the vehicle burst into life, surging forward and away. One policeman shook his fist in impotent fury while the other, slightly more intelligent, wrote down the registration number of the vanishing vehicle. Although this exercise was about as practical as the fist waving: the car had been stolen.

Within seconds the police would turn around and see me there. One last push and I would be off. To think of another plan.

I slammed my shoulder hard against the door in anger—just as it opened. Off-balance I plummeted through and heard it slam behind me.

"Welcome to Castle Penoso, Sir Hector," a tremulous voice said. "Welcome."

I climbed to my feet and dusted off my knees. The owner of the voice stood just before me. A wraithlike gray man with gray hair and gray skin that neatly matched the color of his clothes. I accepted the tremulous hand and pressed the ancient fingers lightly, bowing at the same time. Trying to remember what you called a duke. Your worship? Your highness? Your dukeness? My mind was empty. I would have to fake it.

"What kindness! How can I thank you? I have faced death this day and have only been saved by your timely actions!"

"All I did was open the door, Sir Hector," he said, dismissing this brave action as a mere bagatelle. He blinked rheumy eyes in my direction. "But sit, I pray you, have a drop of brandy. Then tell me everything. I had only a brief note from the marquéz asking me to admit you. He said you would explain."

I did. While schnozzling into the excellent brandy. Of course, I simplified the story in the telling, but the events pretty much followed those that had happened the day before. The duke's eyes widened at my tale, and he trembled and gasped so hard I was worried for him. But he lasted the course and the story so impressed him that he joined me in a brandy.

"Terrible! Terrible! Zapilote must be done away with once and for all. But how is my dear fourth cousin thirteen times removed?" It was my turn to bobble my head, until I finally realized that he must have meant the marquéz; I wondered how they kept track of the family connections.

"I don't know. That is where you must help me. If I write the message will you send it on the semaphore?"

"Oh dear, instantly of course. I will call my operator."

While he tingled his little bell and issued instructions I scratched out a concise query

> I AM SAFE IN CASTLE PENOSO. WHAT IS
> CONDITION OF MARQUÉZ, JAMES AND
> BOLIVAR?
>   SIR HECTOR HARAPO

The duke nodded over the slip of paper and handed it to his operator who hurried off: no long stair climbs for the duke. All we could do then was wait. I made free use of the brandy decanter. When the answer finally arrived I tore it from the operator's fingers, then grated my teeth when I saw that it was still in code.

I paced and muttered while the duke clicked his little wheels and nattered cabalistically to himself. When he finally turned around with the decoded message I was there, behind him, leaning over his shoulder, unmindful of any breach of etiquette. Had they made it through to the castle?

I could feel the tension draining away as I read.

> MARQUÉZ RESPONDING WELL TO MEDICAL
> ATTENTION. BOLIVAR AND JAMES
> UNHARMED. PLEASE ISSUE ORDERS.
>   LADY HARAPO

All was well! The boys had done their job and brought de Torres home. I had seen the medical setup in the castle so I knew that once the doctors and machines had pounced on him he would be all right. And Angelina had taken over in my absence. I could now afford to relax. And I did. By pouring another brandy.

"Good news indeed," the duke quavered. "What will your next course of action be?"

"A careful one. We were lucky to get out alive, walking into the lion's den like that. We won't let that happen again. This campaign must be planned step by step, run like a military operation. Whenever I, and the marquéz, appear in public we are going to be guarded like the crown jewels."

"Yes, the crown jewels. What a tragedy. I remember it like yesterday, when Zapilote had just taken office." Yesterday? That was a good hundred and seventy-five years ago! The General-President wasn't the only one on geriatric drugs. "He promised a rule of law and like fools we believed him. I'll guard the crown jewels he said. Never been seen since. Must have sold them, I know his type . . ."

He rambled on some more like this and I tuned out. What *was* the next step? Getting out of Primoroso and back to the safety of the castle would be a good beginning. But how? I could think of nothing, my mind was empty, my limbs fatigued. I was also half-smashed on the brandy, which might have had something to do with my lack of inspiration. But there must be a special law of destiny that looks after stainless steel rats and other miscreants. Because at that very moment, while I and the duke were both muttering to ourselves through the brandy fumes, salvation was on its way. In the form of a timid knock on the door, repeated again when there was no response.

"Eh, what?" the duke said, rousing from his senile alcoholic revery. "Come in, come in."

The door to the study trembled open and the butler, old enough to be the duke's father, stumbled through.

"It is not my wish to disturb Your Grace," he tremoloed in fine imitation of his master, "but today is Thursday."

"Is there any particular reason why you are giving me this report on the calendar?" the duke asked, head bobbing in wonderment.

"Yes, Your Grace. You ordered me to inform you of this fact every Thursday at least a half an hour before they arrived."

"*Merda!*" His Grace snarled quite gracefully, his rictus of anger revealing a fine set of artificial white choppers. "They'll be here soon."

"They?" I shook my head, feeling I had missed something important.

"Every Thursday. Can't avoid it. Government order. And the fees go against taxes. Tour of noble homes. Filthy off-world tourists trampling through these hallowed halls made sacred by generations of Penosos . . ."

There was more like this—but I wasn't listening. Tourists! Here! All fatigue and most of the effects of the brandy vanished on the instant. Escape from my predicament had just been offered to me on a gilded platter. The silver bell was on the table and I tinkled it loudly, which brought both the attention of the duke and the return of the butler.

"Do I understand that you will soon have oafish offworld tourists shambling through this castle?"

"Indeed, Sir Hector. What terrible times these are."

"They certainly are. How many will there be in the party?"

"There is usually a coach-load from Puerto Azul. Between forty and fifty."

"Invasion of proletarians," the duke adumbrated.

"What precautions do you take to see that they don't lift the ducal silver and paw the paintings?"

"A number of footmen accompany the party at all times."

"Made to order," I chortled, rubbing my hands together briskly as I turned to the duke. "Might I enlist the aid of your staff to assist me in departing this fine castle without drawing any police attention?"

"Of course, anything for the next President of Paraiso-Aqui." He lurched to his feet and placed his hand over his heart, then nodded to the butler who did the same.

"To the next President of Paraiso-aqui," they intoned fervently and I bowed my head at the honor. This little ceremony over with, they were more than ready to help.

"One question first." Their gray heads nodded eagerly. "Is there a secret passage leading out of this castle?"

"There is a secret passage leading out of *every* castle!" the duke said, startled at my ignorance. "Ours comes up in a building across the road. Dug by the third duke. Used to be a brothel there." He smiled faintly, perhaps trying to remember what girls were like.

"Excellent. Then here is my plan. A footman's uniform will

be obtained for me and I will don it. I will then accompany the tourists and choose one to replace. It will be a simple matter for me to then exit with the tourists whose presence will guarantee my safety."

"But your clothes . . ." the duke protested.

"I'll use the tourist's clothes."

"Your beard?"

"Will be shaved off."

By this time the duke had caught on to the idea and was cackling with glee. "How intelligent you are, Hector. You were so stupid as a child I never believed you would ever stop drooling. And the secret passage, of course, we use that to dump the tourist's body into a refuse barrel."

"No bodies!" I said sharply. "If the tourist is killed the investigation will surely reveal that he vanished here. There can be no suspicion. I'll give the man an injection that will affect his memory. When the police find him wandering around, smelling strongly of ron, which I'm sure you can arrange, he will remember nothing of the events of this day. In addition to sloshing him with cheap booze you will also stuff this wad of money into his pocket so there will be no suspicion of robbery. The authorities will laugh and return him to the resort and that will be the end of it."

"I wish we could kill somebody," the duke pouted.

"Later. After the election. Meanwhile I must get that uniform."

By the time I had stripped off the beard yet another time—it was getting a bit ratty after this treatment—and pulled on the knee breeches and other servile clothing, the tourists had arrived. I could hear them chattering like demented squirrels as I slipped into the ranks of the servants. The staff had been told of the plan—and they all proved to be exceedingly well-trained. Not one eye turned in my direction as we plodded in silence after the bare-kneed, loudly dressed, camera-bearing tourist brigade.

". . . *trebonegan eksemplon de la pentroj de la ekskrementepoko de pasinta jarcento . . .*" the guide rattled on, pointing out the badly painted and worse hung portraits that littered the walls. The tourists looked at the paintings and I looked at them, closing in on my kill. Most of the offworlders came in octogenarian pairs and these I ignored. There were some single women trudging along but I passed these by as well, not being up to an instant sex change. Then I spotted my prey. Alone, male, almost my size, wearing purple shorts, a gold lace shirt, and a bored scowl. He had a camera around his neck and a straw bag on his arm bearing the printed message I BEEN TO PUERTO AZUL AND ALL I GOT WAS THIS CRUMMY BAG. He would do—oh yes he would! I walked close behind him and when the crowd turned to look at yet one more bad painting I tapped him lightly on the shoulder. He wheeled about, scowl deepening. I bent to whisper in his ear.

"Please don't tell the others, but there is a free bottle of ron for you. Gift of the duke. One per tourist party. You are the chosen one today. Please follow me."

And he did. Being very careful that the others did not notice him go. Oh, avarice, what crimes are committed in thy name.

"In here, sir."

I opened the study door, and there was the butler holding a silver tray complete with rum bottle. The tourist yakked enthusiastically and extended his arm. I hit it with a slaphypo, then closed the door as he crumpled to the carpet. The duke looked on happily, no doubt seeing this minor triumph as the harbinger of a better age. Who knows, perhaps it was.

I mixed with the crowd, unnoticed in the rush for seats on the bus. A bored policeman counted heads as we streamed from the castle, made a check mark in his book and signaled the driver. The bus doors closed, the air conditioner came on at the same time as the canned music, and we rolled down the road.

The woman in the seat next to me glared at me suspiciously. "I ain't never seen you before," she said.

18

Had I been discovered already? If I silenced her the unconscious body would surely draw attention to me. What could I do? While all these considerations rushed around in my skull I fought a little rearguard action to gain some time.

"Well I ain't never seen you before either!" was my snappy rejoinder.

"Now ain't that something," she simpered, and I realized that what I had thought was suspicion was really passion— and that I was in the process of being picked up. "My name's Joyella and I come from Phigerinadon II . . ."

The sentence ended in an interogative silence and I seized the clue.

"Isn't that a coincidence. My name is Wurble and I come from Blodgett."

"What's a coincidence about that?"

"Both planets are in the same galaxy."

She greeted this limp sally with a whinny of delight and I knew that I had made a friend. Joyella's only problem was that she was getting a little long in the tooth and was lonely. A bit of understanding on my part went a long way and I nodded and tssked through the rest of the journey, as I heard all about life in the accounting department of Lushflush, the robot lavatory attendant factory where she worked. It was late afternoon when we rolled back into the tourist haven of Puerto Azul. Since leaving the duke it had been an alcohol-free day so we nipped into the bar for a couple of tall cold ones. We had had a good day and I slipped out of Joyella's life, ignoring the tremble of her lower lip, before things got too complicated. I shouldered my repellent tourist bag, now well filled with my own equipment, waved goodby, and vanished into the twilight. Next step; getting out of this place. Jorge would know a way.

Except that Jorge appeared to be in a little trouble himself.

I suspected this when I saw the black car drawn up before the doorway of his apartment building. The man slumped behind the wheel wore dark glasses. There were lots of other tenants in the apartment building, it could be any one of them. Then why were the hairs on the nape of my neck trying to rise up out of my shirt collar? My hunches had been right too often in the past to ignore one this time. It would not hurt to take a few precautions. I palmed a slaphypo as I took a map out of my bag. I strolled over to the car and leaned in the window.

"Excuse me old buddy, but I'm looking for this here place. I hear they got good booze and really nifty girls there . . ."

"*No parolas, me, Esperanto . . .*"

"Can't understand a word, old buddy. But just look at the map."

I opened it under his nose and he pushed it away—then slumped in slumber as the needle went home. I leaned his head back in the corner as though he were resting. With my flank secured I turned to the apartment building. Just as two of the Ultimados emerged dragging a much-battered Jorge between them. I stepped forward and halted in front of them.

"Say, that man looks sick!" I said.

"Out of the way, fool," the big one said, reaching out to push me aside.

"You're attacking a helpless tourist!" I shouted, chopping him hard on the side of the neck, then stepping back so his unconscious body could hit the pavement with a satisfactory thud.

The other Ultimado was trying to pull his gun, but Jorge was making this difficult by hanging onto his arm. I settled this little difficulty by chopping the nerve in the man's arm so the gun dropped from his limp fingers. Since this must have hurt I had mercy and rendered him unconscious with a quick uppercut.

"I am very happy to see you," Jorge said, trying not to sway too much. He reached into his bloodied mouth and pulled out a tooth, which he stared at gloomily before throwing it away. Then he kicked the unconscious thug hard in the ribs.

"Let's get out of here," I said. "We'll take the car."

"Where are we going?"

"You tell me." I opened the rear door of the police car and stuffed the two unconscious men onto the floor. "Get in with them," I ordered since he was blinking rapidly and did not really seem to be with it. I closed the door behind him, pushed the dozing driver over, then accelerated away. "Any particular direction we should go?"

There was only silence from the rear seat. I looked back to see that Jorge was just as unconscious as the others. They must have given him quite a going over.

"Which leaves everything up to you, James. Again," I told myself, which observation didn't do much good. I was tired and depressed and had been running from the police for far too long now. There was no point in bringing this crew back into town, so I turned onto the coast highway and rolled along in the gathering dusk. Before it got too dark I pulled off onto the shoulder, then bound and gagged the Ultimados with their own clothing. A few cars whirred by, but none of them stopped. I was dragging the last body into the shrubbery when Jorge stirred and groaned. I rooted around in the bag until I found the medkit which I set for a combination stimulant and pain-killer. I gave him a shot, and it looked so good I gave myself one too.

"Do you feel any better?" I asked as he sat up and stretched.

"I do. I must thank you, for everything."

"Do you have any idea of what we should do next to get out of here?" He looked around.

"Where is here?"

"Coast road. A few Ks south of Puerto Azul."

"Can you fly a jet copter?"

"I can fly anything. Why do you ask—do you have one in your pocket?"

"No, but there is a small private airfield a short distance down the coast. There are craft of all sizes there. Of course it is guarded and there are alarms . . ."

My snort was not one of anger, but rather more like that of a warhorse about to go into battle. My fatigue was gone, I was flying from the uppers, and looking forward to one last quick round of breaking and entering and mugging before taking off for home. It had really been a busy couple of days.

Jorge tried to help, but I instructed him to remain in the car since he would only be in my way. I shorted the alarm in the barbed-wire fence, went over it silent as a snake—and within ten minutes came strolling back to unlock the gate.

"You make it look so simple," Jorge said with justified admiration as we drove into the field.

"Each man to his trade," I murmured deprecatorily. "I'm

sure that I would make a rotten tourist guide. Now we will leave the car here out of sight, and take that sport copter. Don't trip over the bodies, that's right."

By the time he had his seatbelt buckled I had hot-wired the ignition, fired up the engines and turned on the navigation circuitry. I tapped the illuminated map projection.

"We'll head for Primoroso—then turn sharply here over the Barrier and on to the marquéz's castle. Are you ready?"

He nodded and we lifted into the air.

It was an easy flight. Not a single blip appeared on our radar and there wasn't even a disturbance when we crossed the Barrier. I maintained radio silence until Castle de la Rosa appeared on the screen, then identified myself and brought the ship in. The landing pad was brightly lit, and in this welcoming illumination there awaited the three most important people in the galaxy. Important to me, that is.

I dropped from the copter and, with a quick wave to my sons, embraced their mother in such a satisfactory fashion that they clapped encouragement.

"I've been missing that," Angelina said, holding me away at arm's length. "They haven't hurt you, have they? If they have, this planet is going to be littered with corpses very quickly."

"Desist, my love! If anything the opposite is true. I have cut a mean swath through the ranks of the enemy, have won many a fiercely fought contest, have gained us new friends and comrades, cheated at cards, and generally kept myself quite busy while I have been away. How has it been here?"

"Very quiet. The marquéz is recovering nicely, so the boys and I have used the opportunity to make detailed plans."

"Plans of what?" The drugs were wearing off, fatigue struck and I stifled a yawn.

"Plans for you to conduct the crookedest election campaign in the history of electoral politics. It will be a watershed of illegality, a monument of chicanery, a cacophony of corruption."

Jorge stared with disbelief as the rest of us cheered enthusiastically.

19

We sat on the balcony in the glorious morning sunlight, the ruins of our breakfast whisked away by silent servants, sipping a last bit of coffee to hold everything down. It was Angelina, ever practical, who finally touched her lips daintily with her napkin and got down to work.

"While you were away I took the opportunity of going through the marquéz's library. One of his predecessors had the hobby of collecting universities. There must be nearly a thousand of them."

This is not an ordinary hobby, and might even be called an eccentric one. Though it is certainly easy enough to do if you have the money. Not that a university itself costs that much; one of them will fit on a solid-state disc that you can hold on the palm of your hand. It shouldn't cost more than a bottle of rum. The expense comes in traveling about the galaxy, to all of the out-of-the-way planets, to root around in secondhand memory shops and find any old universities that they might have.

"I went through all the university libraries and cross-referenced everything that I could find cataloged on illicit elections and dirty politics. There were plenty of listings, but all of the books I dipped into just complained about this sort of nastiness and how to prevent it without going into details."

"Most unsatisfactory."

"Indeed. Until I ran this incredibly ancient university. The chip was cracked and gray with age, the name of the school itself illegible. It was so old it might actually have come from Earth. In any case the library was almost intact, and in it I found the book that we will use as our bible. I did a printout of it."

She took a heavy sheaf of typescript from the floor, and passed it over to me.

"*How to Win Elections*," I read. "Subtitled, *Or How to*

Vote the Cemetery, by Seamus O'Neill. What can that subtitle possibly mean?"

"Read on. It is a technique that we will be using soon ourselves, where every name from every tombstone is entered into the voting register."

I read on as instructed—and my enthusiasm grew with every sentence.

"Joy!" I said. "Simply incredible. The man's a genius. You are a genius as well, my sweet, for discovering this. We cannot fail."

"Nor shall we. The boys have already begun preparations and we should be able to launch the campaign within a week. Barring unforseen accidents the election is as good as in the bag. And our biggest asset will be General-President Zapilote himself."

"You wouldn't care to explain that. Perhaps I'm being a little dense today . . ."

"He will aid us because of the way he has run his campaigns in the past. Since he controls all the media he has simply gone through the reflex of a campaign. Recorded speeches on television, sycophantic praise in the newspapers, and an overwhelming vote from the electronic polling booths which are rigged to give him ninety percent of the votes no matter how they are cast."

"And that is going to help us?"

"Of course," she said sweetly, smiling indulgently at me as one would upon a moronic child. "We shall electronically usurp the television, print our own editions of the newspapers—and rig the polling booths on the side of righteousness."

Well you can't argue with anything like that. I could only nod in agreement, finish my coffee, then retire to the makeup box and put on my black Harapo beard. While I was doing this I did a speed read through O'Neill's book. It was a revelation. If he were alive today he would surely be elected galactic president; if there were no such title he would have to invent it. My previous reference book for political chicanery was *The Education of a Prince* by Mac O'Velly. But this was a nursery primer compared to O'Neill's masterpiece. When I was bearded and costumed for my Harapo role I summoned a consul of war. The campaign was about to begin. My family gathered around in eager anticipation, and only de Torres looked concerned about the future.

"This meeting is called to order," I announced. "As presidential candidate of the Nobles and Peasants and Workers Party, I intend to make a few appointments. Bolivar, you are secretary of the new party. So please fire up your recorder and take notes. James is rally organizer—which job I will explain in a moment. It is my hope that Angelina diGriz will accept the position of campaign manager, which position also includes the task of getting out the women's vote as well. Do you accept?" I counted the nodding heads and nodded in return. "Good. That appears to take care of the appointments."

"Not quite," de Torres said. "I have another and most important one to make, if I might?"

"Of course—you're the vice-presidential candidate. If I've missed something, please let me know."

He clapped his hands and the door opened. A slight and unassuming man entered and bowed slightly in our direction.

"This is Edwin Rodriguez," de Torres said. "He will be the presidential bodyguard and will accompany you everywhere. We must not have a repeat of the near-disaster that happened in Primoroso. Rodriguez will guard you, detect and eliminate assassins and generally look after your good health."

I looked the man up and down and tried not to smile. "Thank you, marquéz. But while I appreciate the thought I can take care of myself. And I'm afraid this youth might get hurt . . ."

"Rodriquez," the marquéz said. "An assassin at the window!"

My ears rang from the sound of the shots—and I realized that I was lying on the floor under the table and that Rodriguez was kneeling on my back. There was a sizeable and smoking revolver in his hand which was pointed at the window. Most of which had been blown away by the flurry of well-placed shots.

"The attack is over," de Torres said, and the weight was removed from my back. I stood and dusted off my trousers and regained my chair. The marquéz nodded approval. "Just a small demonstration. Rodriguez is my master-at-arms. I sent for him after he became planetary martial arts champion, as well as winning first place in the small arms competition. I have never regretted that decision."

"Nor will I," I said, looking at the now motionless form of my new protector. "I appreciate the thought. And I am pretty sure that he will have plenty to do once the campaign begins. Which will be within a few days. We must catch

Zapilote off-balance and keep him that way. We will begin with an election rally."

"And just what is that?" de Torres asked.

"A form of religious revival meeting where speeches are made, babies kissed, free food and drink consumed by the potential voters. A mixture of carnival, worship and bribery. We will make promises, attack the present regime, and see to it that we have excellent press coverage."

The marquéz shook his head. "It will be suicide. There will be guns, assassination attempts. Zapilote will not let us get away with it. I know the man. He is perfectly capable of dropping a tactical atom bomb on this rally to make sure he gets rid of us. He would take out an entire city to make sure he eliminated the competition."

I smiled and nodded. "I agree completely. Therefore we will not hold the rally in Primoroso, or Ciudad Aguilella or any of the other major cities. Instead we shall hold the first meeting in the small and undistinguished seaside resort of Puerto Azul."

"Why there?" The marquéz was puzzled. Angelina caught on instantly and clapped her hands with pleasure.

"It will be held there because that little town is stuffed full of offplanet tourists. This will guarantee our protection since he cannot permit any of them to be hurt. Nor will he commit any violence in their presence. It is the perfect place for a rally. My husband is certainly using his brains."

I nodded my thanks for the compliment, as well as for the fact that she had not added 'for a change'.

"How do we get there without being blown up on the way?" James asked. This was indeed a problem.

"A good question. Do we go by road or by air?"

"Air would be wisest," the marquéz said. "Once past the Barrier, Zapilote's forces control the roads. We would have to fight our way through. But he has only a few fighter planes and no other air force to speak of. He has never needed one. He controls all the air traffic, owns all the aircraft, other than the few copters and transports that our people have."

"But he could mount an air attack?"

"It is conceivable. There are police gunships in addition to the fighters."

"We'll take precautions." I pointed at Bolivar. "Make a note to use the MES to amplify some weapon systems and early warning detection apparatus. If they do try anything funny we'll get them first."

"As good as done, Dad—I mean President."

"All right. The next order of business is a venue for the colligation . . ."

"You're not even a politician yet," Angelina said, "but you're talking like one already."

"Sorry. It must be catching. I mean, at what place will we hold the rally?"

"There is a large stadium in Puerto Azul," de Torres said. "That is where the bull fights are held every Sunday."

"Bull fights?" I asked. It sounded nasty.

"Yes. It is an interesting taurine event. It features mutated bulls wearing boxing gloves . . ."

"Sounds nice. We must go some time. But for the present we need the stadium for our rally. Which must be kept a secret until the last moment. Any suggestions?"

"Let Jorge arrange it," Angelina said. "He was a tourist guide there so he will know whom to contact. We'll book it in the name of a front organization, a folklorico display for the tourists or something like that."

"Perfect. Then we swoop down during the day, stay in one of the tourist hotels, make speeches on street corners, distribute free tickets to all the voters. And the campaign is launched. Any more suggestions? No? Then I declare this meeting closed and suggest we all repair to the garden for a drink before lunch."

"Champagne," the marquéz announced firmly. "To toast a successful campaign. And to mark the end to this era of misrule."

20

Our little armada left at dawn, four jetcopters and an ancient fixed-wing aircraft that was stuffed full of our campaign supplies. The sun shone, the day was perfect—until a few minutes after we crossed the Barrier when two blips appeared at the very limit of our radar detection screen.

"They're on a convergent track, Dad," Bolivar said, running the reading through the computer. He was in charge of the detection instrumentation; his brother manned our defenses. I looked at the approaching blips and turned on the radio.

"This is the Marquéz de la Rosa flight calling two aircraft now approaching our position. Please identify yourself."

I waited impatiently for a reply but the airwaves were silent. The blips closed in quickly. "Blow them out of the air before they can fire at us!" the marquéz said, fists clenched, glaring at the screen. I shook my head.

"They must attack us first. The cameras are recording all this and I want the record absolutely clear that if there is any violence that we were merely defending ourselves."

"Those words will make a fine epitaph for our tombstones. They are within range!"

"They've fired missiles!" James announced, touching buttons in quick succession. "Counter-missiles launched. Look there, about two o'clock, you'll see the result."

Sudden white clouds burst into silent existence, then fell behind us as the flight moved on.

"Attack craft turning away," Bolivar said. They were all looking at me. I could not speak. "They're escaping, almost out of range."

The marquéz's harsh words broke the silence.

"*Fire!* Take them out."

James's finger was poised over the firing button and it slammed down by reflex at the order. I turned away and looked out of the forward windows. Trying not see the two

109

gouts of red flame exploding off to one side. I was aware of Angelina behind me, her hands on my arms, her voice so low that only I could hear it.

"I understand—and I love you for it. But you must understand our feelings as well. They tried to murder us. And would have tried it again if they had not been stopped. It was self-defense."

I worked to keep the bitterness out of my voice. "I understand only too well. But that's not the way I want it, not the way existence should be. The killing . . ."

"Will be over after the election. That's why you are running for president. To replace the man who ordered this action."

There was no point in any further discussion. I suppose we were both right from our own points of view. The paid killers who had flown those craft would kill no longer. And Angelina was right—the only way to permanently end this violence was to win the election.

"Let me look at my speech again," I said. "I want to get it memorized perfectly." Angelina turned away in silence—but her parting kiss on my cheek spoke volumes.

That was the last of our airborne problems. The blue ocean soon came into view, then the white buildings of Puerto Azul. The campaign fleet circled above the field while our copter with the detection instruments made a sweep of the area. When all of the instrument readings were zero, we came in. I pointed to the row of pink tourist rental cars lined up at the edge of the field.

"Everything in order so far. Let's roll!"

And roll we did, rolling the votemobile out of the open tail of the cargo plane. This had been the marquéz's most luxurious saloon. It still was—plus a few additions. It was now a brilliant white with red-lettered HARAPO FOR PRESIDENT on one side, and HARAPO'S THE ONE! on the other. An overpowered PA system played martial music while it was on the move, and there was an elevated platform where the rear seat had been. The marquéz and I would ride there, waving at the crowd, with nothing between us and them except thin air. And an invisible force field that would block any laser beams aimed at us, would slow and stop bullets as well.

Within a few minutes our equipment and supplies were loaded into the rental cars and our little victory parade rolled away.

"Let's do it in style," I said. "Let them know that a new day is beginning!" A flick of a switch changed the ear-shattering broadcast from marching music to our presidential theme song. We rolled towards the city with its inspiring words booming out around us.

Glory, glory to the workers!
Glory, glory to the peasants!
Down with Zapilote's bullies,
Harapo's marching on!

I can't claim that it was the world's most inspiring lyric, but I doubt if any of the voters would even notice the sprung rhythm as they listened to the shocking words. It was probably a shooting offense to speak out against Zapilote in public. Which meant that even this revolting song would surely capture the listeners' undivided attention.

We got it too, as soon as we left the highway and started driving through the suburbs. Silent, frightened eyes watched us as we rolled by. Only the children cheered and ran alongside when we passed out bags of candy attached to HARAPO RULES OK! flags. Once they ate the candy, they shouted and waved the flags in hopes of getting more. It was only when we swung into the main thoroughfare that we found our first trouble.

A large black police car blocked our way. Filled with scowling uglies who fingered riot guns in a singularly menacing manner. Our little cavalcade stopped and Bolivar walked forward, smiling ingratiatingly, to face the unsmiling officer who stood beside the car.

"Harapo for president," Bolivar said as he pinned an election button on the officer's chest. The man ripped it off and threw it to the ground.

"Go back. Get out of here. You cannot pass."

"Pray tell me why not?" Bolivar asked, offering more badges to the policemen who sneered and pushed them away. Behind him Angelina had descended from the car as well, and was passing out more candy and flags to the crowds of children.

"You do not have a parade permit," the policeman snarled.

"We are not a parade. Just a few old friends out for a drive . . ."

"If I say you are a parade, you are a parade. Now I give

you exactly ten seconds to turn around and get out of here or else."

"Or else what?"

"Or else I'm going to shoot you—that's what!"

A hush fell at these words—and within an instant the street was empty, just a few tattered flags lying on the ground to show that anyone had ever been there. With her audience gone, Angelina went around the police personnel carrier, and offered her flags to the officers there.

"You are going to shoot us—for no reason?" Bolivar said, turning his profile towards us and hamming it up something terrible. Knowing that the whole scene was being recorded. "You would shoot helpless citizens of your own country—you who are sworn to uphold the law!" He fell back and gasped.

"Your time is up. All right men—ready—aim . . ."

A single policeman raised his gun, then slumped down to join his cataleptic companions. Because in addition to the flags Angelina had been passing out sleep gas capsules.

"Fire!" the officer said—and nothing happened. He turned and gasped—then tried to tear his pistol out of its holster. Another broken capsule puffed out its invisible message and he dropped out of sight to join his troops.

As he vanished there was a muffled cheer from the surrounding buildings and the children reappeared, shouting and waving their flags with joy. This time there were more than a few adults with them. There were echoing ha-has of jolly laughter as we pinned a Harapo button onto each police uniform, put a Harapo flag into each dozing hand. After this, happy volunteers rolled aside the vehicle with its unconscious minions of the law; cheers were raised again as the parade continued. More than candy was being given out now. Attached to the flags were the crisp green rectangles of Election Money. Each bill could be exchanged for a bottle of wine and a fried bean sandwich at the evening rally. Things were really beginning to come together.

But Zapilote was still trying to take them apart. As we drove into the center of the city the crowds grew larger, the cheering louder. The marquéz and I stood in the back of the car, waving, while the election anthem rolled out in ear-destroying waves. The stalwart form of my watchdog, Rodriguez, walked alongside the slowly moving vehicle, his grim face grimmer than usual because I had made him leave his recoilless caliber 50 automatic at home. This precaution had been a wise one because I saw him scratching at his empty armpit just as a number of bullets impacted the force field. It was disconcerting to see them suddenly appear before my face, moving slower and slower until they stopped.

"He's in that window on the second floor!" Rodriguez said, pointing. I saw a flash of movement that vanished as I looked. "Go get him!" I said.

Rodriguez hurled himself through the crowd like a surfer through the waves—then on into the building. I ordered the car to stop as I reached out and caught the still-hot slugs as they oozed out of the force field. Dropping them on the floor at my feet. I touched my lapel microphone and spoke.

"Did you get that on tape?" I asked, then looked at James in the following car. He raised the camera and patted it as his radioed voice whispered in my earplug receiver.

"In the can, Dad!"

"Good. Keep shooting. We have just had an assassination attempt and our faithful watchdog has gone after the gunman. There he is now."

Rodriguez had emerged from the building, a long-barreled weapon in one hand, dragging an unconscious man by the other. The crowd murmured and tried to see what was happening as he pushed through them. I switched on the public address system to distract their attention.

"Lady and gentleman voters of Puerto Azul! It has been my great pleasure to come here to meet you, and I sincerely hope that I will see you all at the monster rally tonight. There will be talks, entertainment, free wine, and bean sandwiches, ice cream for the kiddies and a hundred door prizes, yes indeed. You do not have to pay to participate. But a hundred lucky winners will each take home a dartboard with complete set of darts—and these will not be ordinary dartboards, nosiree. Each of these dartboards has a face on it for a target—and I ask you whose face is it? That's right—you can throw darts at the ugly mush of the old dictator himself, Julio 'The Monster' Zapilote!"

As you can imagine that produced a gasp or two and drew everyone's attention. A few of them looked skywards as though they expected a lightning bolt from the heavens to strike and slay me. The car door opened and Rodriguez pushed the assassin and his gun in onto the floor. I nodded when he rolled the unconscious man over and pointed to his dark glasses. My amplified voice rolled out again.

"Now you may call that pretty strong talk—but I mean it. I'm hopping mad. I came here to conduct a peaceful election campaign and what happens? Why I get shot at, that's what happens!" I let the gasp and murmur roll by then turned up the power. "I'm furious I tell you. Right here in my hand I have one of the bullets that were just fired at me. Right at my feet I have the gunman and his rifle. And you know something funny—even though he was shooting at me from inside that building, this gunman is wearing dark glasses . . ."

The crowd roared and surged forward; I signaled the car to start moving again.

"Stop!" I ordered—and they obeyed. "I can understand how you feel. But you are going to see justice done. I am going to prefer charges against this man in a court of law and we will see if the law of the land is still observed in this fair city."

As soon as we were clear of the press of the crowd we picked up speed, then did not stop again until we got to the hotel. The main reason that the Hotel Gran Parajero had been picked was because of its underground garage. Our little convoy hurtled down into it, and all the other cars circled about mine until the area was declared safe. While this was going on I had gone through the gunman's pockets and had found his identification. He was so stupid that he had actually gone out on this assassination mission and taken this along. I read aloud.

"This says that he is a member of the Federal Health Alteration Committee. What in the world is that?" The marquéz nodded grimly.

"You would not know. But that is the official name of the Ultimados. Killers!"

"But not too good at it." As though to prove my words the unconscious Ultimado came to life and pulled a large knife from his belt. I kicked him in the head and he dropped it and sank back again. I bent and seized him up and threw him over my shoulder. "I'll carry him, de Torres, you bring the gun. The press will be waiting and we will really give them something to write about."

We made an impressive sight as we barged into the main ballroom which had been set up for the press meeting. Cameras whirled and flashed and the crowd of newsmen buzzed and stirred like a hornet's nest. They were all there, newspapers, radio, TV, everything. Now the campaign would really begin.

I dropped the Ultimado onto the floor at my feet, then turned to face the press. I raised a clenched fist over my head and glared out ominously as I leaned close to the waiting microphones.

"Do you know what is in my hand? Bullets. Bullets that were fired at me just a few minutes ago." I threw the slugs down and pointed to the limp figure. "And this is the man who fired those bullets at me—from the very gun that the Marquéz de la Rosa is waving angrily over his head. He is as angry as I am. We have just begun this peaceful and democratic campaign when we have been shot at. And not by any common assassin. I have this creature's ID here. Do you recognize it? He is an Ultimado, one of the criminals employed by the dictator Zapilote. Now you know why you must reject this evil dictator at the ballot box and vote for me!

"For I will bring peace and freedom to Paraiso-Aqui at last. Vote for me and this planet will finally live up to its name. Vote! Vote! Vote!"

The campaign had begun. And when the news came out the entire world would know what was really happening.

21

"Not a mention of any kind!" Angelina fumed. "Nothing in the evening papers, nothing on television—not a single word on the radio. There is a complete news blackout."

"Of course," I said, nodding sagely as I brushed bits of dinner from my beard. "We expected nothing less. Did you have any doubts at all that the press was compromised? But doubts are one thing, proof another. And now we can prove it. We'll see if we can make tomorrow's news just a mite more interesting. But for the moment we must think about the rally. How is it going?"

"The stadium has been filled to overflowing for the last hour and we are running out of bean sandwiches. Viewing screens and loudspeakers have been set up all around the stadium for those who couldn't get in."

"Any tourists in the crowd?"

"A lot of them. They seem to think that the whole thing is a lot of fun."

"It would be a lot less fun if they weren't there. Zapilote must be getting desperate by now. I doubt if he will do anything drastic during the rally with the tourists present. But afterwards . . ."

"You watch your step."

"My love, I have every intention of doing just that. Shall we go?"

We went. With all the defensive screens of the votemobile full on. And other precautions as well. We remained inside the garage until a spotter in the hotel above gave us the go-ahead signal. As soon as this arrived the car gunned out into the street—to slip into the gap between two tourist buses. The offworlders were still my best insurance. When we left the highway at the stadium we picked up an escort of pink outrider cars and continued in convoy as we worked our way through the crowds. There was something new outside the entrance. A flexiglass tent with a dozen or more disgruntled-looking men inside it. A jeering crowd surrounded them and pelted the tent with empty wine bottles and stale bean sandwiches.

"And the significance of this?" I asked James, who came forward to greet us.

"We had an empty stadium to start with because there was this gang of police spies stationed just outside the entrance. They were taking pictures of everyone coming to the rally, which meant a decided drop in public interest. This was cutting down on the attendance as you can well imagine. Bolivar and I convinced them that they should give us the cameras and then get into that tent."

"Don't tell me how you did it—I'm a man of peace. Was this the only hitch?"

"The only one. Are you ready for your grand entrance, Dad? I mean Sir Harapo."

"Never felt more ready. And you, Marquéz?"

"The same. This meeting will go down in history. Proceed!"

I did. Down the aisle through the cheering crowd, shaking my hands over my head, smiling for the tourists' cameras, blowing kisses at the babies—but not the babes, for I knew Angelina's steely gaze was upon me. Climbing to the platform and waiting for the shouting to die away. There was a splendid fanfare of recorded trumpets and the marquéz stepped forward.

"I am the Marquéz de la Rosa, as everyone knows. It is my pleasure to run for vice-president of this world, under the leadership of my kinsman, Sir Hector Harapo, Knight of the Beeday, gentleman botanist and full-time recluse. Who has left the quiet of his laboratory and gardens to come to the aid of his planet. Without further ado, let me introduce to you the next President of Paraiso-Aqui . . . Sir Hector!"

Screams, whistles, yells, you know the sort of thing. I waved until my arms were tired, then gave the signal for the fanfare again, while at the same time I pressed the floor button with my toe that sent a quick shot of subsonics through the floor of the stadium. This sound could not be heard, but it would produce a depressant effect on everyone present. The crowd was instantly silent, and I saw tears in more than one eye. Must remember to turn down the subsonic volume. I spoke into the waiting silence.

"Men and women voters, welcome visitors from other worlds, I bring you news of great joy." I turned off the depressants

and toed in the stimulants. The crowd began to smile with
great joy even before they heard the news. "Within a few
weeks we are going to have an election. At that time you will
have a chance to vote for me for president. And why should
you vote for me you might ask? Well I'll give you one very
important reason. I'm not Julio Zapilote, that's why!"

That produced a good deal of enthusiastic reaction and I
took the opportunity to pour out some water-flavored gin
from the carafe before me. I took a few good swallows before
I carried on.

"Vote for me and end corruption in high places. Vote for
me and I'll have the Ultimados working as swimming instruc-
tors on a shark farm. Vote for me and see what honest
government can really be like. I promise an ox in every pot, a
gallon of wine in the cupboard, an abolition of all taxes, six
weeks annual holiday with pay, a thirty-hour work week,
retirement with full pay at the age of fifty for every registered
member of the Nobles and Peasants and Workers Party—
volunteers will pass among you handing out membership
forms—free bull fights every Sunday, off-track betting by
licensed bookmakers, plus a few other things that I will think
of soon . . ."

My last words were drowned out by enthusiastic cheering
that had no need of subsonics. If the voting were held at this
moment—and the machines not rigged—I would have received
every vote. I sat down, still waving, then sipped at my
restorative glass.

"Didn't you promise a few things you can't deliver?" Angelina
asked. I nodded.

"No one believes election promises, particularly the politicians who make them. The purpose of the talk and this rally
is just to stir up enthusiasm."

"Well you certainly have done that."

"Good. A few more speeches and we call it a day. Because
we have a busy night's work ahead of us."

And busy indeed it was. The rally finally ended, we fought
our way through the enthusiastic crowds to the cars, then
moved out onto the highway with the other traffic. The
return trip was happily uneventful and no sooner had we
entered the hotel suite than the action began. "Are you ready
boys?" I asked, tearing out great handfuls of beard in my
enthusiasm to get into action.

"We are!" they chorused.

"Then report." I slipped out of my formal clothes and into my fighting gear. Bolivar read from his notes.

"All major news items are issued by the Ministry of Information to the various media. Resident censors monitor the final copy at each newspaper and at the Broadcasting Center. Pre-recorded news goes from there to the satellites for rebroadcast on radio and television."

"How many satellites are there?"

"Eighteen of them, in geostationary orbits. They blanket the planet. Their signals are either received by personal dish antennas or communal piped systems."

"That's the news I have been waiting to hear," I chortled as I zipped up my soft-soled shoes. "We will just have to forget the newspapers for the moment. It would be too much trouble to sabotage each and every one of them. In any case, I'm sure the broadcast media are the most popular. And vulnerable. What we need next are floorplans of the Broadcasting Center and a diagram of their technical setup."

Bolivar handed me the first, James the second. It was almost too much. I coughed away what might have been a sob and hoped they didn't notice the glisten in the old stainless steel rat's eyes. What fine lads they were, how intelligent in the application of their benevolent crookery!

"We've compared one to the other," Bolivar said, flipping through the floorplans, then stabbing down his finger.

"And are pretty sure that we have found the weak spot," James said, finishing the sentence, a finger firmly planted on his diagram. I bent to look as they traced their way through the details.

"These are the microwave transmitters that shoot the signals around the planet for rebroadcast to the satellites that are out of line of sight."

"And here are the two channels coming out of the program section, radio here—TV here . . ."

"They go through these cables located in this conduit—which just happens to have an access door in the basement of the building . . ."

"*Here!*" I added, stabbing down a finger and we all smiled and nodded like fools. "But this will need a sophisticated circuit interrupter that will be small and hard to spot, yet will still enable us to cut off their signals and substitute our own whenever we wish. Now where could we possibly find devices like that?"

James took one from his pocket, Bolivar took out the other.

"Boys, I'm proud of you," I said, and I meant every word of it. The interrupters were flat cannisters, each small enough to fit on the palm of my hand, with a switch and a bundle of thin wires at one end.

"Self-powered," Bolivar said. "Atomic batteries. Run for years. This lead goes to an outside aerial, while these are spliced into the interior circuits. That's all there is to it. When the correct signal is received the material that Zapilote's technicians are sending out is cut off and whatever signal we are broadcasting will go out in its place. They will think that they are sending out their news reports—but instead they will be broadcasting ours."

"That's good," I said. "But only for a one shot. Once their broadcasts have been sabotaged they will shut down and search until they find these. We will have to go though the whole thing again when we make a second broadcast on election eve. And it will be much harder to set this thing up a second time."

James opened a box while I talked and took out two good-sized hunks of electronic apparatus. "We thought you might have that possibility in mind. So we put these together. They're dummies, full of circuit boards and wiring, that we attach in a slightly more obvious location. They have only one function. If they are disturbed or examined in any way, a thermite device inside is actuated that will then burn them to slag."

"A neat bit of misdirection that will certainly work. Now let's get out there and do the job so we can sleep peacefully tonight."

"Dad, Bolivar and I can take care of this ourselves. You must be tired . . ."

"I am. Of being a politician. You wouldn't deprive me of a chance for a little excitement, would you?"

"They would if I could have my way," Angelina said, speaking for the first time. "But I know you too well. So get out there with your delinquent children and crawl around in the sewers or whatever it is you enjoy doing. But don't expect me to wait up for you."

I kissed her firmly for her understanding and we exited into the night. By way of the back stairs and an unmarked car. Nor were we followed. We parked a street away from Broadcasting Center, then made our way into it. I mean we didn't exactly go through the front door, but we did penetrate without too much trouble from the alarm system. We shorted it out and entered unseen through a basement window. After that it was just a matter of finding the right doorway. The sub-basements were filled with fully automated machinery and empty at this time of night. There was one supervisor at his station, but he was easily avoided. The hookup was a simple one, with the dummy circuit boxes concealed by a partition, while the real bits of circuitry were put under the wire bundle and sealed into the flooring.

"Perfect," I said, dusting off my hands and admiring the result of our labors. "Let us now return for a refreshing drink and a look at the substitute programs that our minions are now preparing."

Getting out unseen was just as easily accomplished as had been our entrance. Our car was waiting and there was no one in sight.

I opened the car door and the light came on.

There was a man sitting there, pointing a large pistol at my head and smiling at the same time. Someone very disgustingly familiar.

"So you are Hector Harapo now, and no longer a simple offworld tourist," Captain Oliveira said. "I warned you at our last meeting not to return to this planet. Now that you have been so rash as to come back you can only blame yourself for the consequences."

22

As he spoke these words the street was bathed with eye-searing light. It was a trap—and well sprung. There were searchlights on top of the buildings and troops pouring out of the doorways. All we could do was surrender.

"Please don't shoot!" I shouted. "We surrender. Surrender, my men, that is an order. *Douchan qounboula!*"

I hoped that the boys would remember this repellent alien language—and they did! Although their hands were in the air, like mine, they could still actuate their smoke bomb releases by crossing their wrists—which I had just ordered them to do. The last thing I saw was the cheering sight of them vanishing in the roiling clouds that sprang up all around them.

I hurled myself aside just as Oliveira fired. The bullet whistled by so close that I felt my hair stir in the breeze of its passage. Before he could fire again I flipped one of my own smoke bombs into the car, following it instantly with a sleep capsule.

I doubt if ten seconds had passed since the moment that I had opened the car door. In that brief time things had changed drastically. The street was filled with vision-obscuring smoke and loud with shouted orders, whistles blowing, the roar of engines and the hoarse cries of attacking men.

"Add more smoke and mix it with sleeping gas!" I called out in the same alien language. "I'm going to start a diversion with this car—then you both make a break for it!"

If I could draw all the attention to myself the boys might have a chance. I groped my way into the car, pushed Oliveira's limp body aside, then started the engine. As I kicked it into gear I twisted the wheel away from the boys and stamped down hard on the accelerator. The car jumped forward, picking up speed, the smoke thinned—then vanished to be replaced by searing light. I squinted against the glare and saw that I was about to run down a squad of terrified soldiers.

I dragged on the wheel and missed them by centimeters, still moving at top speed, to plow headlong into an armored car.

It made quite an impact in more ways than one. I found myself bouncing off the windshield and dropping back into the seat. My nose had taken a good knock and was bleeding nicely down the front of my shirt. My brains had been thumped just as well as my nose and I felt that my head was wobbling on my neck. Thinking was difficult and I had just about enough intelligence left to realize that more smoke and sleeping gas would be a good idea. I was hurling the bombs out of the window when the door to the armored car opened just before me. I threw a few smoke and gas grenades in there by reflex.

And all the while I was holding my breath. I had stopped breathing the instant the rush of blood had washed out my nose plugs. If I took a single breath now I would be just as sound asleep as the soldiers and police. But unlike them I would probably wake up dead.

The burning in my chest drove away the groggy sensations as I crawled out of the car on my hands and knees. As I stood up I banged my injured nose into something very hard. It took every effort of will not to gasp in a lungful of the gas-filled air. The object moved as I touched it and I realized that it was the open door of the armored car. Transportation. I climbed painfully into it, pushing aside the invisible body that was blocking the entrance. There were more slumped bodies underfoot and I had to climb over them.

And I had to breathe. But I didn't dare. I groped forward and slammed my head against hard metal. It took an endless period of running my fingers over it before I realized that it was the base of a seat. The driver's seat, mounted high in the front of the car. My groping fingers found the floor-mounted gear shift. It was vibrating—the engine was still running!

I jammed it into gear. The armored car heaved itself forward and began to grind my car into bits. I cursed and pushed and managed to get the thing into reverse. Everything shook about like crazy then we started moving backwards—I had to breathe!

There was light again. I stuck my head out of the door and hoped that the sleeping gas had been left behind with the smoke. I fought not to breathe, but I could not win. I sucked in a shuddering lungful of air.

Nothing happened. Nothing bad that is, the air itself was pleasure beyond description. We were out of the gas. And things were going very well outside I saw as I slammed the door shut. Smoke and confusion, men and vehicles moving in all directions. My own armored car just one among many drawing away from the smoke and gas. Moving backwards, slowly and steadily out of the area. The driver fell to the floor with a satisfying thud when I hauled at him. I was still gasping in the life-restoring air as I climbed into his seat and took over the controls.

My sons were out there in the smoke and confusion and would need every bit of help they could get. I stopped the armored car and checked over the maze of controls before me. One was labeled *forward turret*, which sounded optimistic. I actuated the circuit, swung the guns to maximum elevation, flipped off the safety and pressed the trigger.

It made a very satisfying roar. The car bucked, empty casings rattled down by my feet and I saw troops diving for cover. Perfect! Now for an exciting exit. Still in reverse I jammed down on the accelerator.

A rear-vision screen showed the street behind me, rushing forward at an incredible pace. It was hard to steer in reverse and I found the car weaving from side to side. I jammed down on the horn, flashed the lights and made what I hoped was an interesting exit. A squad of soldiers appeared on the screen, diving for cover as I roared by. Then I was past them and at a crossroads. I cut sharp on the wheel, skidded to a stop, then jammed the thing into forward gear. Before I could move three more armored cars charged by in front of my car. I smiled at the interesting skidding and crashing as they collided with another vehicle that had been trying to follow me. Before they could sort themselves out I stepped hard on the accelerator and drove happily away from all the chaos I had caused.

And all of this time I kept my thoughts away from James and Bolivar back there in the darkness. They would be all right; they *had* to be all right. I had heard no gunfire from the cloud of smoke. The boys were conscious while the enemy was not. I had created a diversion, there was endless confusion, a number of ways for them to get away. They were smart and strong and would get out of this mess.

Then why was I worried sick and dripping with sweat?

Because I was thinking like a father, not a ruthless interstellar agent. They were my sons and I had got them into this. A black wave of guilt and depression swept over me; I could not keep it at bay. I drove slowly through the dark and empty streets until I finally forced a measure of control through my weepy brain lobes.

"Enough of this, diGriz. Now that you have had a good suffer and a brisk rattle of guilt and self-chastisement—stop it!" I spoke aloud since I can always hear myself better that way. Rather than listening to a thin, tiny inner voice I would much rather hear a big, hearty external one. I sat up straighter and gripped the wheel firmly. "That's better. Moaning and thrashing about and getting yourself in more trouble won't help the boys any. Your task now is to get away safely and back to work and that is all you can do. Now move it."

I moved. Taking as direct route as I could to our hotel. Stopping in a dimly lit street a few blocks short of my destination and abandoning the pilfered vehicle. There was a service entrance, now locked, that admitted me to the hotel at the touch of a picklock. My luck still held out and I rode the service elevator up to our floor without being seen. Angelina opened the door as I approached.

"You look a mess. Are you hurt?"

"Not really. Just bruised and weary. And . . ."

I just did not know how to go on. But my expression must have given me away.

"The boys. What's happened to them?"

"I don't know. I'm sure they're all right. We went different ways. Let me in and I'll tell you what happened."

I told her. Slowly and accurately over large sips of well-aged ron. She sat in cold silence as I talked. Not moving or speaking until I had finished. Then she nodded.

"Racked with guilt, aren't you? It oozes out of your pores llke perspiration."

"I am! My fault. I did it, got them into it . . ."

"Shut up," she suggested, then leaned forward and kissed me on the cheek. "We're all adults and we go into these things with our eyes open. Not only didn't you lead them to destruction, you put yourself in the enemies' gunsights to give them a chance to get away. You did all that you could. Now all we can do is wait. After I patch up that repulsively

bloody nose of yours. I was putting off taking care of it until
you had enough ron inside of you."

I said ouch a few times while she cleaned and bandaged my
nose. Then the waiting began. Angelina, who rarely drank
other than on social occasions, accepted a glass of ron and
sipped at it. There was no conversation. We looked up every
time a siren went by in the street outside. And tried not to
stare at the clock all of the time. I emptied my glass and
reached for the bottle.

"Would you like some more . . ."

The buzzing of the phone cut through my words. Angelina
was answering it before I could move, switching on the
conference function as she lifted the receiver.

"James here," the welcome voice said, and a wave of relief
rushed through me. "No problem getting away. Changed
uniforms with a soldier. But I can't come back to the hotel
looking like this."

"We'll pick you up," Angelina said. "How is Bolivar?"

When there was no instant answer the tension was back.
Multiplied tenfold. He only hesitated for a moment, but that
brief time was message enough.

"I think they have him. I saw police in gas masks driving
off in a great hurry. They were the only ones who left the
scene. I stayed around as long as I could, until the smoke
cleared and they were starting to form the units up. He
didn't call, did he?"

"No. I would have told you."

"I know. I'm sorry . . ."

"You shouldn't be. You did everything that you could. Now
we'll have to make plans to get you back here. Then we'll just
have to wait for news of Bolivar. They won't have harmed
him. I'm sure that he's all right."

Her voice was calm, controlled. Yet I was looking into her
eyes when she spoke and I knew that she was screaming
inside.

23

I closed the ron bottle and put it away; this was the time for a clear head. However I did open a bottle of wine to wash down a fried bean and sausage sandwich since beans are a well known brain food. I think. Angelina went to pick up James while I stared at the telephone. And tried to produce intelligent thoughts about the night's events. By the time they had returned I had reached some highly logical and most unattractive conclusions.

"There were no phone calls," I said as they came through the door.

"If that's food I'll have some," James said, pouring himself a small glass of wine. I was happy that the twins took after their mother in their alcoholic interest, not after their boozer of a father.

"I've made some plans," I announced. "They will guarantee Bolivar's return." Angelina nodded agreement.

"Good. We break into the central jail, shoot down everyone we meet, then release him."

"No. That's what they are expecting us to do. Someone on the enemy team is out-thinking us. We walked into a trap tonight because we were careless. We have been one jump ahead of them so far—and we thought that it would continue to go on like that. But the honeymoon is over. We now have to out-think their out-thinker and do the unexpected."

"Which is what?" Angelina asked.

"Hit them where they don't expect us. Take a prisoner whom we know they will have to trade for Bolivar."

"Who?"

"Zapilote himself. No one else will do."

James was so surprised that he actually stopped eating. Which meant he was very surprised indeed. Angelina had far more control.

"You wouldn't care to explain the tortuous logic that led to that conclusion?" she said.

"I'll be happy to. Somebody on their side has brains. It might very well be Colonel Oliveira. After all he was the one waiting in the car when we returned. Until we find out anything different we must assume that he is our enemy number one. He has been keeping careful track of our operation and has managed to put himself in our shoes. He knows that we must publicize our campaign if we are ever going to get the votes. Nothing of our first meeting with the press was reported, so logically we must then take steps to see that the future will be different. He had no idea of *what* we would do—but he guessed very accurately where we would strike. Broadcast Center. Then he laid a trap that worked—because he succeeded in capturing Bolivar. If he has been right so far he will still be right in assuming that an attempt will be made to free the prisoner. Therefore we can be sure that Bolivar will not be in the local prison. And we can also be sure that the building will be one big trap. We shall stay away from it. And change all the rules of the game. With Zapilote as a hostage Bolivar will have to be released and the score will be nil nil."

"All right so far," Angelina said. "But have you given any thought about ways and means of getting our hands on Zapilote?"

"I have. I am going to get a few hours sleep so I will be fresh for the morning. I will then make certain preparations before I pop over to the capital and look in on the General-President."

"You're insane," Angelina said calmly. "I won't let you do it." She shifted position and a gun suddenly appeared in her hand aimed at me. "That blow on the nose must have addled your brains as well. Go get some sleep while James and I work out another plan that won't be quite as suicidal."

"You would shoot me to save my life? While not denigrating the process in any way, I am forced to admit that the operation of the female mind continues to baffle me. Now put the gun away and relax. It is not suicide I am planning but a well thought-out operation that will extricate both Bolivar and myself from their clutches. Some details are still vague, but I'm sure that they will be clearer after a night's rest."

They were. I woke up at dawn with a flow chart of the operation firmly printed on my frontal lobes. It could not fail!

My good humor continued through my shower and breakfast and the flight to Primoroso and right up to the moment when I was strolling across Freedom Square. It only left me when I entered the grim gates of the Presidio and was stopped by the guard. It was far too late to back out now so I bashed on, good humor or no.

"Where's your pass?" he growled.

"Pass? I need no pass, you microcephalic moron, I am here to see the General-President at the specific request of Colonel Oliveira."

"I am sorry. The Colonel left no orders when he came in . . ."

"Oliveira is here now? Better and better. Get him on the phone. And quickly—if you value your life and sanity."

He was shaking as he punched a number into the phone. The plate lit up and I could see Oliveira's sadistic face on the screen. Before the guard could speak I pushed him aside and leaned close.

"Oliveira," I snarled. "I'm at the front entrance. Aren't you interested in seeing me?"

He did a beautiful take; I should have brought a camera. He had undoubtedly expected a number of possible reactions to the events of the previous evening—but this one was certainly not included. He finally got his eyes back in his head and the blood back into his skin and screeched into the phone.

"Hold that man . . ."

I broke the connection and sat down in the guard's chair. "See how delighted he was?" I took out a cigar and lit it and had barely puffed out the first cloud of smoke before Oliveira came plunging down the stairs with a squad of soldiers at his heels.

"You took one of my men last night," I said, blowing smoke into his face. "I've come to order his release."

As can be easily imagined he did not take kindly at all to this treatment. I made no resistance when the soldiers seized me and hustled me deep into the bowels of the building. Oliveira personally supervised the security procedures, watching closely as I was stripped, searched, X-rayed, body-scanned and purged. He knew that there had to be method in my madness of surrendering to him—but he could not figure out what it was. Then he had the entire security procedure done a second time just in case. Of course they found nothing.

When it was all finished I was given thin slippers and a paper prison suit, then chained heavily at my ankles and wrists. Only after this had been done did he have me dragged to the interrogation room and thrown into a hard chair. He stood over me, slapping a weighted club against the palm of his hand. "Who are you?" he asked.

"I am General James diGriz of the Paramilitary Organization of Political Investigation. You may call me sir."

He struck me sharply across the shin with the club. It should have hurt a good deal. I didn't even notice it. One thing that the examination hadn't shown was that I had been filled to the gills with neocain, a very potent pain-killer. I might not feel very good when it wore off, but for the present nothing could get through.

"No lies and no more of your not so funny jokes. Who are you. The truth this time."

"I've already told you. My name and organization. We of POOPI make it our life's work to right wrongs, to aid in the political growth of backward planets, to help honest politicians like Harapo. To supervize the downfall of criminals like Zapilote."

He struck me again and again and I just sat there and watched him. "Does it give you pleasure to do that?" I finally asked. "If so you must be a very sick man."

He raised the club higher—then threw it away. What good is it to be a bully and a sadist if your victim doesn't even notice it? I nodded approval.

"Now that you have stopped we can converse like adults. My organization is giving aid to Harapo, as I told you. Last night you succeeded in capturing one of my operatives. That will not do. I want him released at once."

"Never! We have him and now we have you and you are both as good as dead . . ."

"More threats? You really are a stupid man." I stood up, very slowly, since it took a greal deal of effort because of the heavy chains. "I shall just have to go over your head. I will see Zapilote now."

"I'll kill you!" he frothed, grabbing up the club again and raising it over his head.

"If you do, Zapilote will have you shot on the spot. My organization will continue to work without me and he will lose the election. Because of your stupidity. Is that what you want?"

He stood there, club raised, trembling, lusting to beat my brains out, but knowing that if he did that he might very well be dead as well. In the end he had to lower it. I nodded approval.

"That's better. We will now go to see the General-President so I can tell him of a compromise plan that I am sure will please him."

"What is it?"

"You will discover that if he permits your presence during our discussion. Call him."

Oliveira was neatly impaled on the horns of a dilemma, and I enjoyed watching him twitch there. He wanted to kill me, or at least to maim me—but he didn't dare. What I had said about Zapilote was true. In the end he realized that and stamped out of the room. I dropped back into the chair and looked gloomily at the bruises that were beginning to appear on my body and tried not to think what I was going to feel like when the neocain wore off. There was a suspicious soft spot on the side of my chest where a rib or two was broken. It was then that I decided that something really loathsome had to happen to Colonel Oliveira before this affair was through. While I was brooding over his fate he returned with a squad of soldiers.

I was hauled to my feet. The soldiers formed a solid wall around me as we marched off down the hall, up a stairway, very tiring, and through a number of anterooms to face a pair of large gilt doors. It had armed guards, weapons ready, stationed on each side. We were getting close to the holy of holies. The doors swung wide, my personal bodyguards pushed me forward, staying so close that I had to peek over their shoulders to assure myself that we were indeed in the Presence. The General-President squatted in a chair like a loathsome toad, his bandy arms resting on an immense desk.

"Tell me about this person," Zapilote said. Still as frog-mouthed and ugly as the first time I had met him. If he recognized me as a beardless Harapo he wasn't letting on.

"He gave his name as General James diGriz," Oliveira said. "And claims to represent an organization named POOPI . . ."

"I'll have you shot if you are trying to make bad jokes!"

"No, please, it is true your excellency!" I enjoyed watching the colonel sweat and tremble. "There must be some truth in what he says. This Paramilitary Organization of Political Investigation that he talks about could exist. Without a doubt he is

an offplanet agent. He came here first some months ago
disguised as a tourist, to make contact with a traitor organization in Puerto Azul. I had him deported before he could
cause any more trouble. He has since returned here illegally
and is very high up in the Harapo organization that is causing
us . . . some little problems . . ."

"I will kill Harapo. Hang him. With his own intestines!"

"Yes, all of the traitors, every one of them, lots of intestines!" Oliveira slavered. "Guts galore . . ."

"Close your mouth, Oliveira, or you'll be first." There was
a crackling sound as Oliveira slammed his mouth shut. I think
he broke a tooth. Zapilote was glaring at me now, his beady
red eyes trying to burn holes through me. "So you work for
Harapo. You cause me all kinds of troubles. Now, before I
kill you, tell me why you came here."

"To make an agreement with you . . ."

"I do not deal with traitors. Take him out and shoot him."

The soldiers closed in, seizing me. It wasn't going quite as
I had planned. "Wait!" I shouted. "Listen to me first. Would
I have come here, alone and unarmed without a reason? That
would be suicide. I came here in order to tell you . . ."
What? I hadn't the slightest idea. But he was listening. What
I had to tell him had to be important. What would interest
him? What does a paranoid dictator care about? *Paranoia!* "I
have come to tell you that there is a traitor very close to you.
Plotting against you."

"*Who?*"

I had his attention now. He was on his feet, leaning across
the desk. "Mrmtrmblmble . . ." I mumbled.

"What?"

"Shall I speak his name aloud, here? With these men
listening?"

"Speak up? Who is it? Tell me!" he frothed, coming around
the desk.

"I'll tell you," I said, bending my knees and tensing my
muscles. "Someone very close to you who wants to kill
you . . ."

And as I spoke the words I hurled myself forward. Smash-
ing into the guards who stood between us, knocking them
aside. Staggering with the weight of the chains, dragging my
arms up. My outstretched hands could barely reach his face;
one fingernail brushed his skin.

Then the blows struck my head and body, driving me to

the ground where the soldiers began to kick me. I was only vaguely aware of Oliveira stopping them, bending over and dragging me to my feet. Soldiers held me tightly; I could barely breathe. Oliveira had his pistol out and the cold muzzle was pushed between my eyes.

"Speak!" he commanded. "One last time before I blow your brains out. Who wants to kill the General-President?"

"I do," I said hoarsely through my bruised throat. "I want to kill him and I have just done so. Don't you see that scratch on his face, the drops of blood?"

Zapilote raised his hand to his cheek and touched it, then looked at the red stain on his fingers.

"You searched me!" I shouted, "But you did not find the weapon. This nail, this fingernail, cut to a point. And coated with four-hour virus. Zapilote has been infected and will be dead within that time. You're dead now, old man. Dead!"

24

As you can well imagine, that made quite an impression on everyone present. Particularly Zapilote. His parchment skin went even whiter and he staggered back clutching at his face. You would think that after having lived for over two centuries he would have had enough of it. He hadn't. He must have got into the habit. I spoke sharply now, too well aware of the gun against my head.

"You're dead Zapilote—if you don't get the antidote in time. Now get this idiot with the gun away from me!"

Zapilote staggered forward and reached up to seize Oliveira's ear, twisting it savagely as he hauled the man aside. The colonel shrieked and dropped the gun—which luckily didn't go off—and clapped his hands to the now-bloody ear. Zapilote shouldered him aside and stood before me.

"Get him on his knees!" Zapilote ordered, and the soldiers kicked me in the legs and forced me down. He stood before me, glaring down, while his breath rich with garlic and heartburn washed over me. "What about the antidote?" he breathed redolently.

"Only I know where it is. If you receive the injection within three hours you will live. The virus that is now spreading through your bloodstream is unknown on this planet. Your doctors cannot help you. By now you should be feeling the first symptoms of the infection. You have a fever. It will keep rising until your brain is destroyed by its heat. Your fingers are now beginning to tingle. Soon they will be paralyzed and this paralysis will spread to your entire body . . ."

He screamed a shrill, old man's scream. Raising his shaking hand to his face, bringing the tremulous fingers away wet with perspiration. Then he screeched again and staggered— two soldiers seized him before he could fall and half-carried him to his chair behind the oversize desk.

"Tell these men to release me," I ordered. "They will take

these chains off me and then they will leave. The creature Oliveira will stay in order to carry out your commands. Issue your orders."

Zapilote's voice quavered as he spoke. The chains dropped away and I dragged myself to a chair and dropped into it. Oliveira stood, dazed, his hands still over his torn ear.

"Here are your instructions, Oliveira. You will get on the telephone at once and issue orders to release the prisoner you captured last night. The prisoner will not be harmed. He will be taken to Harapo's suit at the Hotel Gran Parajero in Puerto Azul. When he is safely there he will be given a phone number that will connect directly with this office. When I have received a phone call from him that I find satisfactory we will discuss the antidote. The longer you delay . . ."

"Do it!" Zapilote screeched. He turned to me as Oliveira worked frantically at the phone. "The antidote, where is it? I am burning up."

"You won't die for over three hours yet. Though you will be very sick. The antidote is nearby. It will be delivered when a message is telephoned. That message will not be sent until I am safely out of here."

"Who are you?"

"Your destiny, old man. Your nemesis. The power that will bring you low. Now send for my clothes so I won't have to waste any of your lifetime later on. See, Oliveira is off the phone. Order him to take care of it."

"How can I believe that you will do this, that you will send the antidote?"

"You can't. But you have no other choice, do you? Now issue the orders."

The entire operation took almost two hours. Two hours in which Zapilote almost sank into a coma due to his rising fever. Two doctors kept his temperature down with antipyretics. But they could not stop the paralysis of his extremities. All sensation and control was now gone from his hands and feet. He screeched weakly when the phone finally rang and I bent to pick it up.

"This is diGriz speaking."

"*Are you all right?*" Angelina asked.

"I'm just fine. How is Bolivar?"

"*He's right here beside me. Eating. Now get out of there!*"

"I'm on my way."

I slammed the phone down and walked through the door without a backward glance. Following my instructions there was a chauffeured car waiting outside in Freedom Square, door open, motor running. As soon as I was seated it hurtled forward in the direction of the airport. My jetcopter was there, fueled and ready. I took off, circled and headed north to meet the heavily armed command copter with James at the controls. He waved to me as he swung his craft up beside mine and his voice echoed in my headphones.

"You did it, Dad! There's nothing in the sky—and if anything does appear we can blast it."

"Good. Send the signal to Zapilote with the name and address of the doctor in Primoroso—then let's head for home. It has been a long day."

I had visited the doctor on the way to the Presidio that morning: it seemed at least a hundred years ago. A very large sum of money had obtained his exclusive services for the day. He had a hypodermic syringe filled and ready and just waited for someone to come and get him and bring him to the person to be injected. I knew that he would get a very warm welcome indeed.

We were joined by the rest of our tiny aerial fleet halfway back to Castle de la Rosa. They had pulled out and left Puerto Azul as soon as Bolivar had returned. None of us wanted to be within range after Zapilote had received the injection and had recovered. We landed together. I killed the ignition and climbed stiffly down from the copter; my side was beginning to ache. Bolivar was standing there when I turned around. He had bruises on his face and I could see a bandage under his shirt. He noticed my attention and smiled.

"Not bad. Just a little kicking around when they caught me. You look a lot worse."

"I'll feel a lot worse if I don't get a little shot of painkiller soon. Take me to your medkit!"

"I have some here. Mom told me about the plan, what you did." His face was hidden as he gave me the injection. "I really do appreciate it, Dad—I don't really know how to say this . . ."

"Then don't. You'd do the same for me. Now lead me to a soft chair and a strong drink and I'll tell you all about my visit to the lion's den. Not the ribs!" I called as Angelina ran up to embrace me. "Let us just sit quiet for a bit before the doc straps them up. They've lasted this long. You know, it has really been one of those days!"

The marquéz must have been told of my arrival as well because he was the next one to rush up arms outspread to embrace me. James stopped him before he managed to puncture one of my lungs with a broken bone.

"Let us take this party inside," I ordered.

"Champagne!" de Torres shouted. At this rate he would be running out soon. "The best in the cellar. The crucial hours of this day will be talked about for years, a century from now!" Which, even if a little confused in its syntax, was emotionally understandable.

We sat in the deep chairs and raised our glasses. It really was the best champagne in the cellar I realized as it spread happiness and warmth throughout my system. I sipped again, and had my glass topped up before I told them the story of my visit to the Presidio. Leaving out the gory bits and making it sound far more exciting than it really had been, which is the way to tell a story.

". . . after the phone call I just walked out of there and into the car. I took off and you know the rest of what happened then. We ended up here."

"Incredible!" de Torres gasped. "What formidable courage to go into that den of murderers like that."

"You would do the same for your son, wouldn't you?" I asked.

He nodded. "Of course. But I did not do it and you did. And what bravery to carry death at your fingertip. But is it not dangerous to travel to the planets, carrying this deadly virus with you . . ."

He stopped and looked around at us as though we were all insane as my family burst into wild laughter. Angelina leaned forward and patted his hand to reassure him.

"It is not you that we are laughing at, marquéz, but at Zapilote. The best part of this is that my Jim would never kill anyone. He couldn't carry through a plot like this if there were the slightest chance that even an animal like Zapilote might die by accident."

The marquéz blinked in confusion. "I do not understand?"

"There is no deadly virus. The fingernail was coated with a pyretogen and a neural anesthetic. One of them gave Zapilote a high fever, the other numbed his extremities. The effects of both of these drugs wear off in about four hours. That's why the deadline."

"But the doctor—the injection?"

"Just sterile water. Now do you see the beauty of it all? It was just bluff! Not only is my husband the world's greatest hero, but he is also the galaxy's greatest con man and actor at the same time!"

I lowered my head in false modesty. But what she had said was true and I did not find it too hard to take. It had been a long, hard day and so a little soothing of the ego was very much in order.

25

I reluctantly spent a rather painful evening, since the effects of the neocain had to wear off before the doctor could treat my bruises and contusions. And broken ribs. Three of them had been fractured by the Colonel, and I sat there and cursed and thought evil thoughts about him while the medic shot bone rejuvenator into the rib marrow, then bound me up. When he was finally finished, a small shot of neocain and a large ron kicked me off to dreamland for some well-deserved rest.

Angelina let me sleep late the next morning, and did not look in until I was taking my second cup of coffee from the bedside dispenser.

"And how are we feeling today?" she asked cheerily.

"I don't know how we are feeling but I are feeling like I have been drawn through a knothole."

"Poor dear," she said, brushing my tousled hair and kissing me lightly on the forehead. "The boys have prepared a surprise that should take your mind off your troubles."

Even as she said this the door opened and James entered carrying a projection TV set. Bolivar was right behind him with the screen. I scowled with instant distrust.

"I hate the box," I animositied. "Particularly moronic morning cretin fodder." Angelina patted my head soothingly.

"There, there, mustn't get irritated. It is not morning TV because it is no longer morning but early afternoon. The traditional time on this planet for the big midday meal. Which is also traditionally followed by the news broadcast watched by almost everyone as they relax, comatose, fingers laced over distended stomach."

"My fingers are clutched to my starving stomach. And I hate news broadcasts."

"Here comes the maid with your nine-course breakfast," Bolivar said, stepping aside so the laden table could pass.

"And this is no normal broadcast either. After the trap that was laid for us outside of the Broadcasting Center we can be pretty sure that we were backtracked. Which means that the dummy interrupters were surely found. But James ran a circuit check last night and the real interrupters are still in place. It took us most of the night to get the tape ready—but we think that you will really enjoy the news today."

"I will, I will," I enthused through a mouth full of food. "And I take back all of my earlier, surlier suggestions. I should have known. Angelina my love, sit beside me and help yourself to a chop and we will enjoy the show together."

The program that preceded the news was just ending as I ended my meal. It was a romantic opera of the kind that mental cripples are said to enjoy, with all kinds of fat people singing into each others faces, clumsy stabbings with collapsible swords followed by hearty songs from the death bed. Happily it ended just as I was reaching for something to throw at the set. A series of repulsive commercials followed, of which only the ron advertisement was bearable, all dewy glasses and clinking ice cubes. But even the most dreadful commercial must come to its sodden end. An off-key fanfare heralded the news and a smart-looking girl swam into focus.

"Good afternoon ladies and gentlemen. This is the afternoon news that is brought to you every day at this time. We have been getting reports from the capital that General-President Zapilote is feeling much better after the mild attack of food poisoning he suffered yesterday. Dear General-President, all of us here, and I know all of you out there, join in wishing you the speedy of speediest of speedy recoveries . . ."

At this point James pressed the button on the radio-control box he was carrying. The screen shimmered for a second and the girl was replaced by a photograph of me, complete with beard, waving enthusiastically and flashing pearly teeth. The marquéz stood at my shoulder. A woman's voice continued the narration—but not that of the previous speaker. I recognized Angelina's voice in an instant and gave her hand a squeeze.

"But let us not dwell on the psychosomatic illnesses of this sordid little dictator, let us instead meet the noble man who will be our next president. I refer to none other than Sir Hector Harapo, shown here with the vice-president to be, the Marquéz de la Rosa. These handsome and noble gentlemen have just held their first election rally in Puerto Azul. It was an enormous success despite the attempts of Zapilote's corrupt police force to prevent it. The first attempt occurred . . ."

It was a snappy production and I enjoyed every moment of it. All the film had been edited to show the opposition in the worst possible light, while our team were unto gods. I clapped enthusiastically when it came to the end.

"Well done! My congratulations to you all. And I would pay a thousand credits to see the expression on that poxy dictator's face at this very moment! But enough. Having finished the first part of the campaign we must look forward to the final stages. We have three months until election day and every moment must be taken up with bringing our message to the people."

"Without any of us getting shot or blown up," Angelina said firmly.

"I could not agree more. But our message must be carried by the news media, and I would welcome suggestions on how that will be done. We can assume that our little TV tap is now being tracked down and destroyed. Once they find out what we have done our chances of fixing any other interrupters into their circuitry are less than zero. But we must have access to the news media or we have lost the election in advance. Any suggestions?"

"The answer seems fairly obvious," Angelina said. "You must interrupt the broadcasting circuitry at the most vulnerable point, which is at the same time the most inaccessible point. If you understand what I mean."

"I don't understand," I admitted unhappily. "I must have been hit on the head once too often yesterday."

"Mom's right!" James said; he had not been hit on the head at all, so was therefore far ahead of me and Bolivar who was also blinking in a concussed manner. "We put the interrupters into the satellites themselves!"

Yes, the answer was hideously obvious and I should have guessed; I pouted unnoticed in the corner as James rattled on enthusiastically.

"The next step then must be a major effort to find out more about the satellites . . ."

"Already done," Angelina said brightly. "There is a company named Radiodifundir SA that is located at the spaceport near Puerto Azul. They service the communication and weather satellites for the government. They are a small company, so small that all of their work is done by a single and ancient spacetug that has been modified for satellite work."

Warm smiles greeted this bit of information, and we all beamed enthusiastically at one another. Being of the same mind and possessed by the same idea. I expressed the thought that was on all our lips.

"It couldn't be that this is the only ship on this planet that can do this kind of work?"

"Not only could it be—it certainly is! If this ship, the *Populacho*, was out of action it would be some months at least before another could be found, modified and brought here."

I rubbed my hands together in anticipation. "The next step is painfully clear. Relay units must be constructed, designed for installation on each satellite. They must be self-powered and will operate when they receive our coded signal. In that manner we can give all the listeners and viewers an unbiased view of the news every day. The ship, the *Populacho*, must be pressed into our service to enable us to install the devices. After which it must be rendered, shall we say, 'unfit' for awhile. At least until the election is over. Can anyone fault this plan?"

"I can't," Angelina said. "But I have one additional suggestion. We are fighting this election in the name of democracy so we must begin acting by the democratic rules we profess to believe in. We must not repeat what we did tonight, cancelling their news program and substituting our own. Democracy means free speech. We must allow them to broadcast, then follow with our own news. The public must be given a choice. People must be allowed to make their own minds up."

"Is that wise?" I asked. "Can they be trusted?"

"Yes, it is wise, my dear husband, though you might not think so. Your personal beliefs fall somewhere between fascism and anarchy. Of the two I favor the anarchy. But given a wider choice I would settle for democracy. All in favor?"

The boys raised their hands and I scowled.

"The ayes have it. We will now plan to commit a crime in the name of the greater good of democracy."

"Who's the fascist-anarchist now?" I growled.

"Not us," Angelina smiled in sweet answer. "We're just pragmatists. Our hearts are pure and our motives of the best. And the results of our actions will be for the greater good of all."

"Say that to the owners of the *Populacho*," I snarled, "when they find their spaceship at the bottom of a smoking crater."

But she was unflappable. "They will get recompense from their insurers and buy a new and better ship. Isn't that what you always say?"

There was of course no answer to that other than to bite savagely into a piece of toast. But even as I chewed I smiled. "You are a fine crew and I cannot argue with you. Now let us extremely honest, democratic republicans, staunch upholders of law and order, begin planning our crime of spaceship rustling."

26

"How does it look?" I said, leaning out of the car window and calling up to Bolivar who sat on the roof above me with the high-power binoculars.

"They're sealing the loading hatch now, so they should be ready for takeoff soon. Wait—yes—one of the crew has just come down and disconnected the power leads, which means that the ship is on internal power. The ground crew is driving away."

"Perfect. Get into the car and we go into action."

He hit the pavement and bounced into the front seat. Bolivar put the car into motion the instant the door was closed. I sat in the back and admired Angelina, sitting at my side, clearly visible as soon as we had pulled out of the darkness of the hangar into the glare of the spaceport lights.

"You're adorable! I just love your kinky white nurse's out-fit. If only you had brought a white whip with you."

"Do you really like it?" she asked, ignoring the crude flagellation funny. "The skirt isn't too short?"

"Very short—and very nice," I said, patting the neat turn of white thigh between skirt and knee. "The idea is to distract these people while we work our will upon them. And you are the most distracting thing on this planet."

"You're not to shabby yourself with that uniform and curly moustache."

I twisted the ends of this hirsute object, then gave the rows of medals on my chest a jingle. "Everyone respects authority. So the more authoritarian you look the more respect you get. All right team, here we are. Operation Medico will now swing into action."

We climbed from the car at the foot of the gangway and I led the way up to the entrance, light gleaming from my high-peaked cap and pristine uniform. Nurse Angelina fol-lowed and the boys brought up the rear, white-suited and lugging a great white case. The crewman, on guard at the ship's airlock, gaped in appreciation, then grew resolute and barred our way.

"You can't go in here. Due for takeoff in a couple of minutes."

I looked him up and down slowly with the same expression on my face that would have been there if he had just wriggled out from under a flat rock. As a worried look crossed his features I took out a scroll and let it drop open before him. It was covered with fine black and red printing and sealed with a great gold seal. My voice was most stern.

"Do you see this? It is a quarantine document issued by the Board of Health. There is a medical emergency and you will take me to your captain at once. Now—lead the way."

He led. It had really been quite easy. As soon as a turn in the corridor blocked any view he might have had of Bolivar and James, they sealed the airlock behind us. The captain looked up, shocked, when we entered the control room.

"What is going on here! Get out at once . . ."

"You are Captain Ciego de Avila. I have here a quarantine notice from the Board of Health. Your men must be examined before this ship can leave."

"What are those morons in Primoroso trying to do to me!" he protested. "My schedule, do they ever think of that? I have a launch window coming up in less than thirty minutes."

"You will launch on time, I guarantee you. For our sake as well as yours." How true! "We are trying to contain an outbreak of a rare disease brought here from another planet. Perrotonitis . . ."

"I've never heard of that."

"That shows you how rare it is. The first symptoms are fever, slavering and growling like a dog. We have reason to believe that one of your crew is infected."

"Which one?"

"That one," I said pointing at the crewman who had led us here. He whinnied and shied away. "Nurse, examine his throat."

He reluctantly opened his mouth and Angelina pushed down his tongue with a wooden depresser. "His throat is very irritated," she said.

"I'm not sick!" the man wailed, saliva forming at the corners of his mouth as he spoke. He wiped it away with the hot skin of his hand. "Not sick . . ." he growled—then barked twice.

"He has it!" I shouted. "He'll be wagging his tail next! Grab him men and I'll administer the cure!"

Barking and yapping, with Bolivar hanging from one arm and James from the other, he was immobilized so I could give him the injection. Which not only knocked him out but neutralized the reactive agents that he had absorbed through the mucous membranes in his mouth—put there by the tongue depressor.

"Caught in time," I said, looking down at the unconscious body while I put the hypodermic back into its case. "He will recover after he regains consciousness. Now, Captain, order the rest of your crew here at once for examination. If it is done quickly you will make your launch on time."

It was done quickly. Within five minutes most of the crew had developed symptoms and were stretched unconscious on the deck. It was not by chance that only a skeleton engine and control room crew remained. I nodded approval, then took out a large pistol and pointed it at the captain.

"I am now taking over your ship. Long live the revolution!"

"You can't do this—you're mad!"

"No we are not mad, just incredibly vicious. We represent the Black Friday-afternoon Revolutionary Party and we will kill you to make you free. We fear nothing. You will operate this ship in its normal manner or we will murder your crew one by one until you agree to cooperate."

"You're all nut cases! I'm calling the police . . ."

He reached for the radio but I moved faster. Seizing him by the arms and spinning him about.

"Kill the first one," I called out.

"Freedom and liberty!" Bolivar shouted as he pulled a large butcher knife out from under his jacket. He leaped upon the unconscious figure at the far end of the row, kneeling on the man's chest.

Then he bent forward and cut the man's throat with a single vicious swipe of the sharp knife. There was a gurgling cry as the blood spurted out of the awful wound. It was very realistic.

"Take the body away!" I shouted, and turned back to the captain. If I had been impressed—even though I knew that the flesh-colored apparatus filled with blood had been fixed to the front of the man's neck, that the shriek came from an apparatus in the knife—well, you can imagine the effect this had on the captain. He staggered and the blood drained from his space-tanned face. I had made my point.

There were no problems after that. Both captain and crew cooperated to the best of their ability. We cleared for takeoff with spaceport control and lifted into orbit. As we were jockeying into position near the first satellite, the boys opened the crate and extracted one of the self-powered interrupters. I had been studying the wiring diagram of the satellite and had pinpointed the place where it should be connected. The wire leads were color-coded; there would be no problems.

"I'll suit up now," I said.

"Let one of the boys go," Angelina said. "Your ribs aren't healed yet."

"Healed enough to get this job done. There'll be enough work for all of us if we are to install these on every satellite. I want to put the first one in myself in case there are any problems."

"You just want the glory—and the fun of a spacewalk."

"I couldn't agree more. Without a little excitement life would be so dull."

And it was indeed fun. The blue globe of Paraiso-Aqui floated serenely below me, clear and sharp. I admired it briefly, then jetted over to the communication satellite, ducking under the outstretched arms of solar cells and up to the pitted central structure. It was the work of a moment to find the right plate and to swing open the hatch in the thick insulating skin. The carefully constructed cannister slid into the opening, while a few touches of the plasma iron sealed the connecting wires into place.

"Ready for testing," I said into the radio.

"*Right, testing now.*" Nothing was visible since all of the operating mechanisms were solid state and it is not easy to see electrons slipping through circuits. "*Works fine. Cuts in and out just like it should.*"

And so it went. The installation of the interrupter devices was not difficult or time-consuming, but matching orbits was. The ship's computer flashed its little numbers, which were translated into orbital positions, then into firing increments for the jets. The entire job took almost four days to complete and we were all getting more than a bit tired by the end.

"There are dark little satchels under your eyes," Angelina said, pushing the bottle of ron in my direction. "Which in a way rather balances the bloodshot condition of the eyes themselves."

"Well we're just about done. And we can rest when we get back." We had just eaten so a single little ron should do me no harm. Might even help. It had been an exhausting job, because in addition to the work the crew had to be watched and guarded at all times. The boys looked as tired as I did. Only Angelina, who had labored as hard as any of us, showed no sign of stress. Eternal youth! The ron tasted good.

"I wonder how the election campaign is going?" she asked.

"Slowly, I'm sure. But the marquéz is holding the fort and issuing press releases every day—even if no one knows about them. Which situation will change as soon as we get back and put this new system into operation."

"It's still unnerving to be out of touch with things for so long." She poured a tiny ron for herself and sipped it.

"We had no other choice. If the forces of evil knew what we were doing up here they would blast this ship out of the sky. They'll never think that anything is wrong here as long as we stick to routine transmissions, with the radio closed down the rest of the time. What's to worry? The election is still a month away. By election day we will have ninety-nine percent of the voters lined up behind us and it will be a landslide."

"You're right, of course. It must be the fatigue that is putting all these strange fears into my head. After we all have had a bit of rest I'm sure that I'll be all right. I think." She scowled in my direction. "Now don't laugh, Jim diGriz or I'll break both your arms. But I have an intuition that something is very wrong."

She looked at me very closely and I fought down any tendency to laugh, giggle or find fault with her in the slightest. In fact I had no such tendency at all. I shook my head and searched the bottom of the ron glass for an answer.

"Don't you laugh either," I said. "But something is bothering me too. The lack of contact I suppose. Though I can't imagine what could possibly go wrong at this time."

"We'll know in a few hours," she said, most practically. "Now get down to the brig and send James up for his food." As she was saying this the spacesuited Bolivar clumped in, his helmet in his hand.

"Done!" he announced. "The last one is in place. Now Harapo has but to speak and the whole world will listen. Dig

out that moth-eaten beard again, Dad, because you're going
on camera!"

"Best news I ever heard. We're heading home!"

The captain, who still thought we were a gang of killers,
was immensely relieved when he was asked to compute a
landing orbit. Though from the look of fear on his face when I
popped the gas capsule under his nose he must have thought
it was the end. It wasn't. Just sleep gas to keep them all quiet
while we landed the ship. The coded message had been sent
and now it was up to me to bring the ship in for what could
be a difficult landing. "I laugh at difficult landings," I muttered as I punched the new coordinates into the computer.

Our orbit brought us out of the night into a golden dawn,
down through a thin layer of clouds towards the ground
below. Where no spaceport was visible.

"I hope they followed your directions about the hole,"
Angelina said, scowling attractively into the viewscreen.

"It will be there. We can count upon de Torres."

I was right. The dark mouth of the opening yawned in the
middle of the field near the castle. A radio beacon guided us
in, but I cut it off when we were two hundred meters up and
made the delicate part of the landing myself. Jets flaring, my
attention on the radar and lower screens, I dropped the ship
down into the immense hole in the ground. We touched with
the slightest of bumps and I killed all the power.

"Done," I announced. "When the dummy barn is put over
the hole this spaceship will have disappeared. Until after the
election. Though the crew will not have their freedom I am
sure they will appreciate the hospitality here."

We were climbing up to the bow port while I talked. It
swung open at the touch of a button and sunlight streamed
in. A construction crane was just swinging a gangway into
place so we could make a graceful exit. We strolled across it
to greet the marquéz himself, who was waiting at the far end.
But instead of joy and welcome his face was a study in darkest
gloom.

"It is terrible," he said. "A painful tragedy. The end is
upon us."

Angelina and I exchanged a single glance. Had our premo-
nitions of doom been right?

"What's wrong?" I asked.

"You wouldn't know, you were out of touch. All the work
wasted, ruined."

"You wouldn't like to tell me why?" I grated through clenched teeth.

"The election. Zapilote has declared a state of emergency and changed the date. It is taking place tomorrow morning. There is nothing we can possibly do in the little time remaining. He is sure to be re-elected again."

27

If you're holding your breath, why then a day is a long time. But if you are trying to fix an election, then a day is no time at all. And a day was all that we had left.

It is hard to admit defeat, particularly for one like myself who, if you will excuse me saying so, has never been defeated. Nor was I going to be this time!

"It won't work!" I announced loudly. "That putrid politico is not getting away with it."

They stood in awe of this statement, so forcefully and firmly declared. It was only after some hesitation that Bolivar asked the all-important question. "How are you going to stop him?"

How indeed? I hadn't the slightest idea.

"That will be revealed tomorrow. It takes a bigger man than Zapilote to put the skids under Slippery Jim diGriz."

I turned and marched resolutely away before there were any more embarrassing questions. What *was* I going to do? That vital question flickered about in my frontal lobes, and occasionally dropped into my temporal lobe, and once even into my cerebellum, without producing an answer. I returned to our suite where I bathed in perfumed water and scrubbed myself until every pore gleamed. Then I shaved, and brushed my teeth, took an upper—then a downer to get myself off the ceiling—and still no answer was forthcoming. As a last resort I tucked into a healthy breakfast, then washed it down with countless cups of black coffee. Followed by even more coffee laced with ancient ron. The results were no better.

"Face it, Jim," I said, sitting on the balcony and staring out at the view, "you have lost the election."

It was almost a relief to come to that conclusion. It cleared the air. He who fights and pulls his freight, lives to fight another date. Count your losses and get out. Lick your wounds—then return. Because there was just no way that the

151

planet-wide election system could be fixed in a single day. As things stood now it really didn't matter how many people voted for Harapo. Their votes went in one end of the crooked voting machines and votes for Zapilote came out the other.

As soon as I faced this indisputable fact the glimmerings of an idea began tapping faintly for attention. But why? What was important about this bit of bad news? I paced the floor, smoked a cheroot, scratched my head, poured some ron, rubbed my chin and did all of the other things that are supposed to make the brain tick over. One of them must have worked because I was suddenly electrified, leaping into the air and clicking my heels together. Or rather thudding them together, since I was barefoot. I grabbed for the phone and punched in de Torres's personal number. It took a moment for the call to go through, and when his face appeared on the screen it was bouncing up and down with the sky in the background.

"*What is it?*" he asked. There was a regular thudding sound beating time behind his voice. Then I realized that he must have gone riding and that the telephone pickup was in the pommel of the saddle.

"Just a question if you don't mind. This planet is now theoretically an established democracy, isn't it?"

He bounced and nodded. "*Theoretically is the right word. We have a constitution that promises everything, though of course we receive nothing. Our motto should be that there are no fixed rules. Anyone can be bribed, anyone corrupted. On paper, yes, we are a democracy . . .*"

"Well that paper is what I am interested in. Where can I see a copy of this constitution?"

"*In my library. It is in the memory banks, but there is also a bound volume on the stand between the windows. Why do you ask?*"

"All will be revealed very soon. Thanks."

I pulled on some clothes and hurried down to the library, tiptoeing past the tall windows that opened out onto the balcony, because I could see Angelina and the boys having coffee there. It wasn't quite time for explanations yet.

The constitution was just where the marquéz had said. I opened it and groaned. There were over nine thousand pages of fine print. I obviously had my work cut out for me.

There was no point in going through the massive thing page by page and scribbling out handwritten notes. Never keep a dog and bark for yourself; that's one of my mottoes. I turned on the library computer, dredged the constitution up from the memory stacks and punched it into current memory. I then wrote a simple search program and went to pour myself a drink while it began dredging through the massive thing for some nuggets of gold.

It wasn't easy. There did not seem to be much coherence to the constitution. It was written in a half-dozen styles, all of them obfuscatory of course, and contained repetitions and redundancies galore. After awhile I began to see why. It soon became obvious that Zapilote had not written the thing, but instead must have clobbered it together from a number of other documents. This was both good news and bad. Bad in that I had to scan almost every page myself, good because there was such a variety of material. There had to be *something* I could use among all this legal rubbish.

The shadows were lengthening across the floor before I did. A secondary reference to a sub-clause in an appendix relating to additional addenda. I read it once quickly, and as I did I felt a warm glow suffuse my body. Then I went through it again, more slowly, dancing a little jig as the glowing letters moved across the screen.

"*Eureka!*" I cried, unable to contain myself any longer. Then *Eureka!* again as I keyed in the computer's voice simulator, then actuated it to say *Eureka* too. And to repeat itself in a number of different voices and melodies. Within moments a chorus of booming "*Eurekas!*" was filling the air. Angelina appeared at the doorway and lifted one quizzical eyebrow.

"I thought you might have something to do with this insane chorus. Dare I guess? Does it have any bearing on our little problem?"

"Big problem, my sweet!" I said, seizing her hands and dancing her around the room. "A large problem that appeared insoluble until this very minute, though don't tell anyone else that. I would not want to spoil my reputation for infallibility. I have come up with an answer that is so simple I dare not breathe it aloud—to any other than you—in case word might reach the forces of evil that oppose us. They could easily avert disaster if they knew in time what I was planning. But they shall not know—and this evening's news broadcast will be designed to so infuriate Zapilote that he will work his evil will to excess. Come—to the recording studio!"

I am not a sadist at heart, so I really was not overjoyed that our broadcast would spoil many a TV viewer's evening. But I needed prime time for my announcement. The program I planned to interrupt could easily be repeated—though I couldn't imagine why. It was a loathsome series about a family of perverted sadists who ran a boarding kennel cum insane asylum where people could leave off their nutsy relatives when they went on vacation. It was entitled *Ain't Love Grand* and was purported to be watched by one hundred and eight percent of the viewing audience. Some of them were obviously watching it twice.

We finished our recording just in time. The boys had set up and tested the satellite interrupters and they were in perfect working order. Our signal would be broadcast from the dish aerial on the roof, going first to the geostationary satellite in orbit high above us. All of the normal programs would then be shorted out while our program was relayed from one satellite to another, finally to be beamed back to the expectant audiences on the planet below. They were in for a different kind of thrill tonight.

"Three more minutes," James said, slipping the big cassette of tape into the player. "Aren't you afraid of losing your audience, Dad? Won't they turn off their sets when they see that they are getting a political broadcast?"

"Not the way we've written it. They'll be glued to their chairs. Watch and see."

Our homely little family scene was being repeated around the globe. The father turning on the set, then sitting down in the best chair with brimming glass or cup. The mother at his side, doing something domestic like knitting booties or fiddling the tax returns. The children at their feet, the servants in their hovels huddling around their battered machines. All the world awaited breathlessly its favorite program. It began.

And was ruthlessly interrupted just as it got into full sadistic swing. The picture blinked and sputtered and was replaced by a view of Angelina clutching at a microphone. She was wearing the same uniform as those of the regular announcers, while the background was an exact duplicate of the national news studio.

"I have terrible news to bring to you," she said in a horror-filled voice. "There has been an assassination. No, not the loathsome Zapilote, that is almost too much to ask. Presidential candidate Sir Hector Harapo will now tell you what has happened. After his brief talk the regular program will be resumed. Sir Harapo." My bearded image appeared, fist raised for banging down on the table before me.

"Assassination!" I banged. "Do you know what has been assassinated? I'll tell you what. Your free choice, guaranteed under our sacred constitution, to elect the presidential candidate you think is best. That choice has been assassinated. By whom, you ask? By that little worm Zapilote who has eaten away the core of our noble republic, that's who. I have always spoken well of my opponent in this presidential race. I shall do so no longer. I shall name him as the gray-furred, long-whiskered, foul-breathed rat that he is. A rodent gnawing away at the supports of our heroic republic. He flaunts our laws. He tried to prevent me from running for office by secretly closing all nominations—but I out-thought him there. Easy enough to do with a creature that has the IQ of a retarded cockroach. Since his first attempt to stop me was foiled he has tried again. He has moved forward the election date in an attempt to prevent me from meeting you good voters out there, to stop me from telling you of his sins and my abilities. But that shall not be so!"

I stopped for breath and recorded cheering echoed loudly. It faded when I raised my hand.

"You noble voters will have your chance tomorrow. Get out there and vote! Vote for Harapo and de Torres, because every vote for us is a vote for liberty and will bring a bubble of froth to the demented lips of Zapilote the dictator, soon to be deposed. He cannot win! It shall be a landslide for Harapo! Let us sweep the board in order to sweep that loathsome maggot into the dustbin of history! Thank you."

The announcement ended with martial music and snapping flags.

"I get a feeling you don't like this guy, Dad," Bolivar said.

"You're going to make him angry. If he has his way you won't get a single vote," James added.

I stood and went over to my discarded doctor outfit and removed the most ornate medal from it. I bade James rise and pinned it to his broad chest and we all cheered.

"That is an award for clear-eyed vision, my son. You have, as they say, hit the nail squarely on the head."

"Well, thanks, I'll wear it always. Even in the shower. But would you like to clarify a bit just how you can win by losing massively?"

"I'm afraid that must remain a secret between myself and

your mother, for at least a little while longer. No word of my plans must be breathed aloud, even within these castle walls. You shall know, first thing after the returns for the voting come tomorrow. If you can figure out by then just what I am up to—why you get another medal."

28

Election day began with a bang.

The explosion blew out a number of windows in the castle and jolted me in an instant from a deep slumber to a painfully wide-awake condition. I stood by the bed, alertly poised on the balls of my feet, my hands extended in the best karate position.

"Aren't you cold, just standing there like that?" Angelina asked from the warm depths of the covers.

"Yes, now that I think about it, I am," I shivered and dived back in. As I was reaching for her the phone rang and I reached for it instead.

"Must have been a big one," Bolivar said, "because the defense screen is set to take out any offensive action when it is five Ks away. Aerial bomb. Big as a house. Computer back-tracked its trajectory then launched a missile at whatever dropped it. The second explosion was too far away to be heard."

"Thanks for the info," I said, smacking my lips at the sudden bad taste in my mouth. I stood up and wearily pulled on my robe.

"You didn't expect him to exactly send you flowers, not after all the awful names you called him, did you?" Angelina said.

"No. But I didn't want any more lives lost." I looked out at the gray of dawn and felt rather gray myself.

"The new president will stop all the killings forever—that's the way you have to look at it. Now order up some food. It's going to be a busy day."

As indeed it was. After a satisfying but rapid breakfast, followed by a quick check that my beard was firmly in place, I was off to the level meadow behind the castle. All of the cows had been ejected to make room for the tents. The marquéz himself was supervising the operation as they were unloaded from the trucks.

"Good morning, Hector. As you have ordered, the tents are here and are being erected. There is much wonder among the workers—on my part as well—just why we need a carnival at this time. Is it to celebrate the election? Do you think we will win?"

"All will be explained in a few hours, my dear Marquéz. But I dare not breathe a syllable now. But you can tell your men that they can make the job easier by not bothering to erect the grandstands."

"Just empty tents?"

"That's it."

I left him with a look of befuddled bemusement on his face. I was to see that expression more and more as the day wore on. Though they were all to polite to say so, I had the feeling after a few hours that most of the people on the castle staff thought that I was mad. Crazy as a rat, that's what! I laughed a quick chuckle-chuckle under my breath, and went on with the preparations for the day.

The first order of official business was of course registering my own vote. The polling place for the district was in the small town of Tortosa, a few kilometers outside the marquéz's estate. We went there in a convoy of polished cars, election flags flapping in the breeze of our passage. Our arrival was timed for nine in the morning when the polling booth was to be opened. We drove into the central square just as the clock in the town hall was clanging out the hour. A line of prospective voters already stretched across the square.

"A good turnout," de Torres said.

"A good turnout of ward heelers as well," I said, pointing.

There was a large gang of Zapilote's followers grouped about before the entrance to the hall. They waved drab banners with the official colors, sickly green and mud brown, of Zapilote's Happy Buzzard party. They had already worked their way down the line, pinning a Happy Buzzard button on each of the waiting voters.

"We're on stage," I said as my followers grouped behind me. My faithful watchdog, Rodriguez, stood close, as did Bolivar and James. All three were unarmed—but very dangerous. I nodded to Angelina who carried the camera and recording apparatus. "This is it. Roll the camera. Action."

With heavy tread we marched across the square to face the

local mayor, a toady of Zapilote's of course, and the chief of police. They looked nervous and fingered their sidearms.

"The law is being broken here!" I said sternly, pointing an accusing finger at them, keeping my best profile to the camera. "It is forbidden by the constitution to canvass within two hundred meters of the polling place. Eject these men at once!"

"I am mayor here!" the mayor here squeaked, "and I take orders from no one. Chief, send these people packing."

The chief of police was unwise enough to reach for his gun. Rodriguez took one step in his direction. There was a whistle of wind as his hand made a quick pass in the air. The chief was suddenly unconscious and lying on the ground. The Happy Buzzards flocked closely together bleating to one another. I walked in their direction, Rodriguez and the twins at my shoulder, and they broke and ran.

"Remove those disgusting buttons," I ordered. "You, mayor, get in there and open the voting, for I shall cast the first vote for myself."

As soon as he scrambled into the town hall all of the waiting voters cheered and pulled off their Zapilote buttons. There was a rustle like that of falling leaves as they were all hurled out upon the cobbles of the square. My ward heelers, careful to begin their operations a good two hundred meters from the door, began passing out our buttons, the proud symbol of our party, the Avenging Terrier. On the button was a small white-and-brown dog with large teeth holding a dead rat in his jaws. Said dead rat bearing more than a passing resemblance to Zapilote. Everyone wanted a button, and even those voters near the entrance hurried outside the polling limit to get one before going back to their places in the line.

"And now," I announced to the waiting voters—and to the camera, "the voting will begin!"

There was a lot of cheering and cries of "Harapo's the one!" and "The Avenging Terrier will strike!" and this sort of thing as I and de Torres marched into the town hall, followed by our alert bodyguards.

My name was found in the voting register, I signed in the indicated spot with a flourish—then went forward into the polling booth with all eyes upon me. I reached up and pulled the handle that closed the privacy curtain and actuated the machine. Since this was a presidential election there were only two levers on the board. One for each party. I reached out and pressed down the Harapo lever. The mechanism whirred, a panel lit up saying VOTE RECORDED, and the curtain opened behind me. I stepped out and made way for the marquéz.

"And how does this apparatus work?" I asked the election official in charge of the registration book. He looked about, not wanting to be seen talking to me, but could not avoid an answer.

"It is all electronic," he finally said. "Your vote is recorded in the machine's memory bank. When voting is over for the day the central computer automatically connects through to this machine, and one by one to every other machine, and reads the memory and enters it into the central memory bank. When all of the voting stations have been reported in, the final vote is counted and displayed."

"How do we know that the central computer won't cheat? That it hasn't been programmed to let one side win?"

"Impossible!" he said with what appeared to be hearty conviction. "That would be illegal. The man with the most votes will win."

"Well you are looking at him!" I reached out and pumped his reluctant hand. "This is the day when a new broom sweeps clean the foul nest of dictatorship that has locked a slimy metal hand on the bloodstream of the country. Victory!"

Cheered on by this masterpiece of mixed metaphor I exited with de Torres to the cries of the happy voters. We reboarded the cars and swept off towards the castle.

"That's that," I announced. "Nothing more to do until the polls close at six. I hope that the chef has prepared a good lunch."

"No more canvassing?" Bolivar asked.

"No more getting out the loyal voters?" James added. "Unless something is done there is going to be a landslide for Zapilote."

"How interesting," I mused, a secret smile on my lips. "I do hope that there will be a fish course. It goes so well with the white wine."

It was indeed a wonderful lunch and I must admit that I dozed a bit after the liqueurs. Politics can be so trying. The sun was low on the horizon when I opened my eyes—to see Angelina silhouetted most attractively before its radiant disc.

"You're a vision!" I said. "What time is it?"

"Time for you to wake up. I have told the boys everything. They greeted the plan with great joy, and left with the convoy at the appointed time. The polls are just closing now."

"Wonderful," I said, standing and stretching. "Let us go listen to the results."

The forces of darkness wasted no time. The preliminary results were already coming in when we joined the marquéz. He was pacing back and forth, shaking his fist at the TV screen as he went.

"A landslide, that is what they are predicting. That criminal has terrorized the electorate. They are afraid to vote against him."

"I think the answer is really simpler than that. All of his electioneering is just window dressing. He who controls the computer can bring in the final vote any way that he likes. That's why it would have been a waste of time to do any more campaigning."

"Then we have lost."

"I think perhaps we are going to win. It all depends on how angry Zapilote is. Look—this might be the news that we have been waiting for!"

The announcer, a very oily type with a pimp's moustache, was waving a fistful of computer printouts at the camera, while at the same time he was working up a pseudo-enthusiasm.

"This is wonderful, absolutely wonderful. A landslide for our dear General-President. A spontaneous outwelling of loyalty from the people he holds so dear. An affirmation of their faith despite the efforts of wreckers and other vermin to undermine this grateful affection that has grown with the years. Wait—just a moment—yes, the final results have just been handed to me, the results that we all have been waiting for."

"You can say that again," I said, then said it again. The announcer smiled greasily and held up a sheet of paper, then lowered it and read from it.

"The results just in from the town of Tortosa, in the Central Region. This town is next to the estate of an individual named de Torres, the so-called Marquéz de la Rosa. Charges are being pressed against this malignant individual for defamation of character and treason. But meanwhile his name has remained on the voting machines as a vice-presidential candidate, along with that of a sick deviant called Hector Harapo who is so misguided that he thinks he has a chance of being elected president. But we live in a democracy, ladies and gentlemen, where even the lowest can lust for the highest position. And these two are the lowest, let me tell you. In fact—let me prove it! Figures don't lie."

He waved the paper again and I muttered "Get on with it, you cretin." He must have heard me.

"But let us get on with it, the suspense is almost unbearable. In the town of Tortosa, where these thugs voted and used dire threats on the happy villagers to make them vote for them, in what they thought was their very own territory— the results are quite amazing. They are . . . General-President Zapilote . . . five thousand, three-hundred and twelve. While the vote for the traitors Harapo and de Torres is . . ."

He extended the silence for long seconds, before screaming into the microphone.

"*Two!* They voted for themselves—and no one else, not a single person voted for them. This is loyalty indeed. The landslide marches on and there is no doubt now that our dear President will be re-elected by acclamation . . ."

"The swine!" de Torres shouted as he kicked the TV set to bits. "We saw them vote, we know how they voted! Lies, just lies!"

"Of course," I said. "I wouldn't want it any other way." I thumbed on the command radio at my elbow and Bolivar's voice issued from it.

"*All ready here.*"

"Then roll it. The results were even better than we expected."

The marquéz crunched a few last TV components under foot and looked at me as though I were mad.

"We are going to make a broadcast to the world very soon. Just as soon as the convoy returns . . ."

"Convoy?"

"Let me explain. You deserve to hear it before everyone else does. We now have Zapilote exactly where we want him. In his greed for revenge he has played right into our hands!"

29

It was only fair to let the marquéz have the big picture ahead of the rest of the world. He was kicking fitfully at the shattered remains of the TV set when I handed him the computer printout.

"The answer to all our problems is right here in the constitution," I said. "Read this."

He did, with patient attention, word for word. And as he did so his scowl faded away, to be replaced by a wider and wider grin until, at the very end, he burst into a roar of laughter, hurled the printout away and seized me in a bearlike embrace.

"You are a genius, a genius I say!" I did not want to argue, although I did writhe in his grip and eventually managed to escape, but only after he had kissed me fervently on both cheeks. There are some cultures I will never understand. I was so involved in this little drama that Angelina's voice on the radio was a welcome interruption.

"*The convoy is on the grounds now and inside the defense perimeter,*" she said. "*The tapes will be here in a few minutes.*"

"Wonderful! The marquéz and I will slip into our best uniforms so we can fire the final shot after the recordings are played."

We all gathered in the library before the big projection TV. The interrupter link to the satellites was set up and ready to go at the press of a button—and I held the button in my hand. The camera was pointed at me as I stood beside the bound edition of the planetary constitution, my fingertips resting reverently upon the open page. The TV screen was filled with scenes of repulsive enthusiasm as Zapilote's followers indulged in an orgy of self-congratulation. The sound was turned down to a mutter, since looking at this nonsense was bad enough.

"You can turn that off any time you like," Angelina said.

163

"I can, and I will, because I can't take too much of it either. But the Happy Buzzard himself will be sure to speak, and I would love to break in then. Wait—this could be it! Will someone kindly turn up the sound."

The announcer was writhing in an orgasm of pleasure, sweating profusely as he pointed off-camera. ". . . yes, I do believe it is happening. Pandemonium fills the hall as this celestial being who has sacrificed himself so much in the past does us the honor of running again for head of state. He is stepping forward now, the crowd goes wild, weak women faint and strong men have tears in their eyes. He raises his hand for silence and silence instantly falls, the only sounds now the expectant panting of his followers and the thud-thud of a few more women fainting. Ladies and gentlemen, citizens of Paraiso-Aqui, it is my everlasting pleasure to introduce to you General-President Julio Zapilote!"

The screen filled with Happy Buzzard's loathsome features, made even more loathsome for being seen on the large screen. The rat-trap mouth chomped a bit before the slimy syllables rattled forth.

"I expected no less from you faithful voters. The election is over and you have done your duty and voted in the correct manner. We have heard the last of that criminal Hector Harapo . . ."

I pressed the button and his image was instantly replaced with mine.

"The last? You treacherous little lying louse, the fight has yet to be joined! Do you think you can cheat the voters of this fair world by dropping their sacred votes out of the bottom of your crooked voting machines in order to substitute your own illegal results? It shall not be so. You are condemned out of your own mouth. Justice will be done! In your greed you have committed the serious crime that will lay you low. The world will now watch as we take you to the little town of Tortosa. The time, as you can see by the clock in the town hall, is just a few minutes after the polls closed earlier today . . ."

My form did a slow dissolve to be replaced by the town square. James was doing the voice-over.

"The polls are now closed and the citizens of Tortosa are gathering to hear the results. For some reason, perhaps because they are Zapilote supporters, the mayor and the chief of police tried to slip out of town a few minutes ago when they thought they were not being watched. The chief of police is still unconscious, but the mayor is dying to talk to us."

The mayor looked decidedly unhappy as he faced the camera, but Rodriguez's grim presence at his shoulder guaranteed his cooperation.

"Please tell us, Mister Mayor, was the voting orderly and were all the votes carefully recorded in the voting machine?"

"Yes, of course, all was in order." He looked up in concern as the square behind him began to fill with people.

"Will you please tell us, since you are mayor of Tortosa, are these the citizens of your fine town who are gathering here?"

"Yes, most of them I suppose. I can't be sure . . ."

"You can't be sure? And you have been mayor—for how long?"

"Twenty-two years."

"Then you should know these people by sight."

"I can't be sure of all of them."

"You can't? Will you then point out any strangers?"

"There are none that I'm sure of, that I can see."

"Well, we must be sure. Ahh, here is the chief of police now. I'm sure that he can help us. Please tell the audience, chief, how long have you lived in Tortosa?"

"Well . . . all my life." Most reluctantly.

"Good. Then do you see any strangers here?"

He looked around and even more reluctantly said that he didn't.

"Very *good*," James said. "We are just in time for the big event—the election returns are coming in. As a public service the loudspeakers will be turned on so that everyone present can hear the results."

The mayor and the chief of police seemed to shrink inside their clothes when they heard the outcome of the election. When the vote for Tortosa was announced they stirred in panic, but Rodriguez stepped forward and they grew still again. Behind them the good voters of Tortosa roared in protest.

"Did you hear that?" James's voice asked. "Could something be wrong? Just two votes for Sir Hector Harapo—and every other vote for Zapilote. Let us find out for ourselves." A switch was thrown and his voice boomed from all of the loudspeakers. "Good people of Tortosa, this is the representative of Sir Hector speaking. He is of the belief that the repulsive swine of a general-president has thrown your votes away, that the voting machines are crooked, that Zapilote is cheating you out of your representation on this ballot. Let us discover the truth. Will every person here who voted for Sir Hector Harapo please raise his or her hand. Thank you."

Silence filled the square as the hands went up. Slowly, firmly, proudly. A sea of hands. An uplifting demonstration of the truth.

"Very good. Thank you. Will you please lower your hands. Now I ask for the hands of those who voted for Zapilote."

All of the hands dropped. Not one hand lifted. Yes, one, two hands, as the mayor and the chief hesitantly raised their palms. James's voice was jubilant.

"There you have it, people of Paraiso-Aqui. Proof positive of the crime of disfranchisement. All of the people of this town, with two verminous exceptions, have been deprived of their vote. We have positive proof that in Tortosa the voting was fixed. The wrong man won."

I signaled and the camera came back on me. I pointed gravely at the massive tome beside me.

"A crime has been committed. A crime that you will find reference to on page nine thousand and three of the sacred constitution of this planet. The wording of clause seventy-nine on this page is clear, painfully clear. I will read it to you." I raised a copy of the clause and read from it in my most impressive and sonorous voice.

"Due to the nature of electronic voting and due to the necessity of assuring that the voting is always recorded with utmost accuracy and due to the invisibility of the votes once they have been recorded in the voting machine, it is hereby ordained that strictest controls and regulations must be observed as stated in paragraph nineteen, subsection forty of the voting act, and as further guarantee of the surety of the votes it shall be declared and enacted that if it be proven beyond doubt that the record of votes in a single voting machine during a presidential ballot be proven to be substantially altered, then that presidential ballot shall be declared null and void, and all of the ballots cast in that election shall be declared null and void. It is furthermore required that two weeks after this declaration of nullity there shall be another ballot and this ballot will be potentiated using the original system of paper ballots and ballot boxes and the winner of this election will be declared President and he shall instigate an investigation of the voting machines before their next use in any election."

I placed the paper reverently back upon the constitution, then turned slowly to the camera. In a serious and ominous voice I spoke.

"I therefore declare this election null and void. In two weeks' time there will be another election. At that time— may the best man win."

30

"Cut," Angelina said, and there were shouts of joy from all present.

"You have done it," she said, and kissed my cheek above the fuzz line. "And you have taken care of all of the voters of Tortosa as well."

"Absolutely. For our sake, as well as theirs, they are now settling down in their bedrolls in the tents outside. Safe from any retaliations from Zapilote's creatures. They will remain for the two weeks until the next election and will be handsomely paid for their little vacation. All of them seemed to enjoy the idea."

"He will ignore us," de Torres said gloomily. "He will pay no heed to the demand for another election. He has the power to do this."

"He dare not," I said. "It would ruin the planet's economy. Without the import of offworld currency his corrupt and incompetent administration would be bankrupt in a week. I have sent full details on the election to every planet supplying tourists to this world. They will be watching the result with close attention."

"Then we have won!" de Torres said, striking a victorious pose.

"Not yet," I told him. "We have still to fight the battle of the ballot boxes. But this time we will be ready. For every dirty trick he knows I know three. It will be a conflict every step of the way, but at least now we stand a chance.

It was a very busy two weeks. The official ballot boxes were manufactured and sealed under the strictest supervision. But we had little trouble extracting a sample from their warehouse in order to go into the ballot-box business for ourselves. We did the same thing with the ballots, and very quickly had printed as many as had the government presses. I didn't know what kind of dirty tricks they would be trying, so we had to be ready for everything and anything that might come our way.

Nor were we being tardy on the organizational front. Jorge, once a tourist guide and now in charge of our recruiting campaign, had flying squads visiting every polling district. Local volunteers were formed into secret committees, then issued with scrambler radios so we could be in constant touch with all of them. Campaign brochures poured forth from printing presses right around the planet, and we saw to it that there were two news bulletins on radio and television every night. First came the lying government one—then ours followed immediately afterwards. We kept the news factual and accurate and free of political bias. That was enough—it was a breath of fresh air after the drivel that had preceeded it. We knew that their technicians were doing everything they could to jam or trace our signals. To no avail. Freedom of information had come to the planet. If the ballot could be kept relatively honest Zapilote's regime was surely doomed.

We had real proof of this when the government car approached our perimeter defenses on day eleven, just three days before the election. It was stopped by the guards who put a call through to me.

"Excuse me, Sir Hector, but the party in the car will speak to no one but you."

"What's the security status?"

"Detectors reveal only small arms. No bombs, no radiation devices of any kind. One passenger in the back, a driver and guard in the front."

"Sounds good so far. Who is the passenger?"

"We can't tell. The windows are opaqued."

"Let them through. I don't think we'll have any trouble looking after them."

Nor did we. The car was stopped among the trees well away from the castle. Rodriguez and Bolivar had a squad with them; they had the two men who were in the front of the car disarmed and whisked away within seconds. I strolled into sight and looked at the dark windows. I was quite relaxed, possibly because of my superior combat ability, but truthfully because of the portable force field generator that protected me.

"You can come out now," I said.

The door slowly opened and Zapilote poked his head through, then climbed down.

"What an unexpected pleasure," I said.

"None of that nonsense, Harapo. I'm here to talk business."

He reached behind him in the car and removed a metal box. When he turned back with it in his hand my pistol was trained between his little beady eyes.

"Put that away, you moron," he snarled. "I'm not here to try to kill you." He threw a switch on the box and it began to hum loudly. "This is a white noise generator. It blacks out any kind of recording equipment and sets up air tremor patterns that make photography and lipreading impossible. I want no record of this conversation to exist."

"Fine by me." I put the gun away. "What do you want?"

"A deal. You're the only person in a hundred and seventy years that ever gave me a fight. I appreciate that. It was getting kind of boring."

"Not to the people you had beaten to death."

"None of that liberal hogwash for the masses. There are just the two of us here now. You don't care about the microcephalic mob any more than I do . . ."

"What makes you say that?" The conversation was beginning to get interesting.

"Because you are a politician, that's why. The only thing politicians care about is getting elected, then re-elected. You have stood up to me and made your point. It's now time for us to get together and make a deal. I'm not going to live forever, you know . . ."

"That's the best news I have heard yet!"

He ignored me and pressed on.

"My geriatric shots aren't having the same effect that they used to. I may have to retire one of these days. So I'm thinking of bringing someone along to take my place. And that person is you. How's that for an offer?"

He started to cough and had to grope in his pocket for a pill. It was a great offer. On his terms it was incredible indeed. He had built a political machine and had taken over the planet completely. And he was offering me a share in it—and a future of controlling it. It was a magnificent offer. "And what will I have to trade off for this job?"

"Don't be stupid. You lose the election. You take a dive. And after that you stay in politics in opposition to me. Everyone thinks that you are the greatest thing since they invented sex, so all the bleeding-heart liberals flock to your cause. You organize them and see that they don't do any harm. Of course you let us know who the real revolutionaries are so we can dispose of them. This system will last a thousand years. It's a deal, right?"

"Wrong. And I know that I am going to have a job explaining to you exactly why. You see I believe in the one man one vote system . . ."

"Ha, ha!"

"Equality before the law . . ."

"Come off it!"

"Free speech, habeas corpus, no taxation without representation . . ."

"Do you have a fever, Harapo? Just what the hell are you talking about?"

"I said that you wouldn't understand. So let me put it on your terms. I want all the loot and I want it now. I want all the money, all the power, all the women. I intend to kill anyone who gets in my way. Do you understand?"

Zapilote sighed and nodded his head and snuffled. "I'm an old man and I get emotional when I hear talk like that. Reminds me of me at your age. I need you on my team, Harapo. Say you'll join me!"

"I'll kill you first."

"Really wonderful. Just what I would have done." He turned and climbed slowly back into the car. Before he closed the door he looked at me again, sighed and shook his head. "I can't wish you good luck. But I can say that meeting you has been a great emotional experience. I know that after I go my work will be carried on by someone who understands me, who thinks like I do."

The door slammed and I signaled for the return of the other two men. I watched as they climbed in, then drove away.

"What was all that about?" Bolivar asked.

"He offered me the world. A partnership now, and the whole works after he was dead."

"You said yes?"

"My dear son! I may be a crook but I'm not a criminal. It's the Zapilotes in this universe who have to go. The little men with the big contempt for mankind. I may rob a man of his wealth but I would never take away his life or his freedom. In fact I don't rob people of their wealth. I rob corporations, companies, those bloated and insensate creatures that lock up our wealth . . ."

"Dad—I've heard the lecture."

"Right. Let's get back to the castle. I want to wash my hands and get a drink. I don't like the company I have just been keeping."

31

I was up at the crack of dawn on election day, breathing deeply of the morning air just as the sun popped over the horizon.

"Aren't we being energetic so early?" Angelina said, opening one eye to look at the clock, and not liking what she saw.

"This is not the time for slugabeds! History is being made today—and I'm the one who is making it."

"I can't face all that ego so early in the morning." She pulled the blankets over her head. "Go away," she muffled.

I hummed happily to myself as I trotted down the stairs. The marquéz was breaking his fast on the patio and I joined him there.

"History is being made today," he said.

"I just said the same thing myself." We raised our coffee cups and drank a toast to victory. Bolivar and James soon joined us, and by the time the polls opened at nine we were already in contact with our teams in the field.

Within three minutes we had a dozen cries for help. Our poll watchers were being beaten up, two of them had been shot, and four fake voting registers had been discovered. I had expected no less. We did what we could, but our forces were small and thinly spread. And the decision had already been taken to concentrate our strength on the large cities. Our most important weapon was the offworld newsmen. When word of the canceled and fraudulent election had gone out to the planets, great interest had been aroused. A few of the big planetary networks had sent their reporters, but most of them had not had the time to make the arrangements. Therefore most of the newsmen were freelancers, forty-three of them in all.

"It's working," Bolivar said, as he finished a call on the radio. "That was the tenth precinct in Primoroso. We caught them packing the ballot box. One of the newsmen got it all on tape and there is going to be a recount. We're really lucky that so many newsmen came for this election."

"Luck, my son, is never a matter of chance." I humbly averted my eyes. "There are forty-three freelance newsmen here because that was the most I could hire at short notice. Their fares have been paid, they are enjoying their holiday—and anything they may make by selling their material is found money."

"I should have known," he said. "If there is any crooked way of getting a thing done my dad will think of it!"

I slapped him on the shoulder and turned away, too filled with emotion to speak. Praise like this is more precious than pearls.

By midafternoon the fat was really in the fire. We were fighting a rear-guard action and barely holding our own. In some of the smaller towns we knew that we had lost since Zapilote's supporters had simply closed the polls at gunpoint and substituted their own stuffed boxes. We had to let them get away with it. It was the big population centers that counted and we were still managing to hold our own there. With any luck it might be a fairly honest ballot, with a final vote that represented the will of the people.

As the reports came in the marquéz began to grow more and more depressed. He cracked his knuckles pensively and shook his head in anger.

"This is no way to go about it! We do nothing on our own! Our people just sit around looking at the wall until it is too late. Only after the illegal acts have been committed do they go into action. We can never win unless we hit them first and hit them hard. Why don't we just shoot all the Zapilote supporters?"

"My dear marquéz, we *have* to win in the way we are doing it now. Otherwise it would not be a democratic election."

"I'm beginning not to like this democracy of yours. It is too much work. It is much easier to tell the peasants what to do. They like it that way. We know that you will make a better president than that piece of filth Zapilote. So let's just make you president and let it go that."

I sighed deeply. Gonzales de Torres, the Marquéz de la Rosa, had an attitude towards the world that went with his name. He would never understand the reality of democracy. I had to count upon his kindness and personal code of values to get his cooperation.

"I'll explain some other time. Meanwhile we have to set up the automatic ballot box stuffers."

"The *what*?"

"The machines that will return whatever vote we like in the districts we chose."

"You can do this? And if you can do it—why aren't you doing it for all the districts and save a lot of time and effort?"

"Because we must have what at least appears to be an honest election. If our new world starts corruptly it is going to go on being corrupt. However if we have to give it a little corrupt help I intend to keep that a secret from the electors. We want them to think that democracy works—and it *will* work after the election. So what we are doing is keeping track of every ballot box that has been rigged, stuffed or falsified in any way. And we are not interfering with the boxes themselves."

"Then we will lose."

"No we will win. That is guaranteed in each of those districts. Because it is not the boxes that will be interfered with—but the information about those boxes."

"You have lost me," he said, then poured some ron into a glass. "This is said to help the mental processes."

"Well help mine too, thank you. It is really very simple. We are attaching one of these devices to the phone lines of each of the vote-counting officers in each of the affected districts."

I held up a compact metal box with wires coming from it. He looked at it dubiously. "A miracle of microcircuitry and applied chip technology. With this we monitor all calls to a selected number. Eventually the ballots will be counted and a phone call made. The official will then read out the results. As he does this his call will be intercepted and relayed to your big computer here on another phone line. The computer will take the image of the speaker and his voice, break them down into bits, restructure them so the speaker will then give the results we want—and send the corrected image back down the telephone line. This process will take a small amount of time."

"How small? The deception will be detected . . ."

"Not in four milliseconds, four-thousandths of a second, which is all it will take. You have a good computer."

"We should do it for all the ballot results?"

"No, that would be immoral. What we are doing is moral

but illegal. It is a fine point upon which I base my entire existence, which I will attempt to explain to you some day when we have more time. Just a drop more ron—fine, thank you—then back to work."

The results of the ballot would be declared in the Primoroso Opera House, a giant hall that been designed for this occasion. Every four years it was packed with Zapilote's followers, who would do no more than greet the rigged vote with wild applause, then hail victory just one more time. This year there would be two candidates on the platform and the results, hopefully, would be a lot different. We kept working and put off leaving as long as possible, until Angelina and the marqueza forcefully dragged us out to the waiting copter.

"Isn't that a little ornate?" Angelina asked, pointing to all the gold braid and jingling rows of medals on my uniform.

"Not in the slightest. People appreciate a good show. And they like a president to look like a president. Let's go!"

We flew to the city in an armed group, and equally well-armed cars met us at the airport. Zapilote would love to assassinate us if he got a chance so all precautions were taken. Once we entered the opera house we would be all right, since by mutual agreement no weapons would be allowed inside. Zapilote was just as careful of his skin as I was of mine.

He was on the platform ahead of us, and snarled and spat when I waved a cheery greeting.

"Not in a very cheerful mood is he? I hope he has good reason."

It was a great social occasion and the crowd was buzzing with excitement. Champagne was being drunk in great quantities, though between sips all eyes were on the great screen over our heads where the results would be displayed. Right now it read zero zero just like the opening of a ball game.

There was a sudden hush as a bell rang loudly and the chairman of the balloting committee took his position before the microphone.

"The polls are closed and counting will now begin," he said, and everyone cheered. "Here is our first count, just in, from Cucaracha City. Are you there, Cucaracha?"

The screen below the scoreboard cleared and an immense projected face appeared.

"Here is the count from Cucaracha City," the man said, then lowered his eyes to consult the paper in his hand. "For

President Zapilote, sixteen votes. Next, for Sir Harapo . . . nine hundred and eighty-five. Long live Harapo!" But as soon as he had shouted this he looked around worriedly, then vanished from the screen. The marquéz leaned over to me and whispered behind his hand.

"Very good. You would never know that it was a computer talking, not the real man."

"It's even better than that—because that *was* the real man. An honest vote. Let's hope they all come in like that."

But of course they didn't. Zapilote's henchmen had done their work well, so that a number of counts were just as skewed as the first one—only in the opposite direction. Bit by bit the returns mounted—and the tension did as well. Because we were neck and neck. Wherever an honest vote had been recorded the Avenging Terriers ate the Happy Buzzards. Far too often the opposite was true. At times we would be ahead by a whisker, at other times they led by a beak. It was neck and neck.

"It is very exciting," de Torres said. "This election business has more fascination than a bull fight. But it gives one a thirst. I happen to have some ninety-year-old ron in my pocket flask. Would you care to give me an opinion on its quality?"

Without too much urging I gave my opinion and he checked it. There were now only four polling stations to go.

"Are any of these ours?" de Torres whispered.

"I don't know!" I groaned. "I've lost track."

First Zapilote led, then the votes fell to me, then, on the next to last report, he was ahead by seventy-five votes.

"You could have done a better job of cooking the books," Angelina said. "Or simply shot the old buzzard."

"Democracy, my pet. One person, one vote, you know the theory, and the results never known until the very last vote is counted . . ."

"Here it is, ladies and gentlemen, the report is coming in now, the very last report!"

A face filled the screen above our heads and we twisted our necks to look up at it. A man, heavily moustached and gloomy of mien.

"It is my pleasure to bring to you the final ballot from the resort town of Solysombra, garden spot of the south coast . . ." The audience groaned and I gritted my teeth. ". . . the final count is . . . just a moment I have the paper here."

"I want that man killed at once!" Zapilote called out, and the marquéz nodded agreement with the dictator for the first and only time in his life.

"Yes, here it is. It is my pleasure to report that fair Solysombra has awarded eight hundred and nineteen votes to our beloved General-President Zapilote . . ."

"That puts us eight hundred and ninety-four votes behind," Angelina said. "It's still not too late to poison him."

". . . and for the other candidate, what's his name, yes, Harapo, I have the unhappiness to report he has managed to scrape together—my goodness!" His eyes bulged and he looked around and began to sweat. "I must report that he has . . . eight hundred and ninety-six votes."

The crowd went wild as the numbers were flashed on the board. Zapilote was shaking his fist in my direction and Angelina was shouting in my ear.

"You won by two votes! Your own and de Torres's."

"Truth will out!"

I stood and waved back at the audience, clenched my fists over my head, bent and kissed Angelina, shook hands with the marquéz, thumbed my nose at Zapilote who was frothing with rage, then stepped forward to the microphone. I had to stand there for a minute with my hands raised before the pandemonium died down. The cameras were trained on me, the ears of the galaxy waiting eagerly to hear my words. At last I could speak.

"Thank you, my friends, thank you. I am a modest man—" Angelina clapped loudly at that, which started the audience off again. I nodded and smiled and waited patiently for the applause to die away again.

"As I was saying, I am a modest man and do not thrust myself forward. But the public will has spoken and I will answer it. You have my promise . . ."

I'm not sure if I heard the shot, but the impact of the bullet hurled me backwards. My chin dropped to my chest and I saw the red blood pumping out, spreading.

I was falling. Falling into oblivion . . .

Afterword

There might possibly be someone, someplace in one of the more backward parts of this planet, who might not know me. My name is Ricard Gonzales de Torres y Alvarez, Marquéz de la Rosa. I have been asked by the official historians of Paraiso-Aqui to record the events of that black day. Though I am no writer by trade, I consider it a repulsive and degenerate occupation for a grown man, I nevertheless agreed, since I am the person obviously best suited to the task. The men of the de Torres family have never shirked their responsibilities, no matter how onerous they might be. Therefore I begin at the beginning, where I am told all stories should begin.

I was sitting just behind that wonderful man, that paragon of all virtue, the noble Sir Hector Harapo, Knight of the Beeday, gentleman, scientist and loving father. I can not praise him too highly. But I digress. I was sitting next to him when he spoke to the audience, to the world—the entire galaxy—at that moment of our greatest joy. That repellent slug Zapilote had been defeated in an honest and democratic election. Hector was President and I the Vice-president-elect. The world was going to be a better place.

Then the shot was fired. It came from high in the building, from one of the small windows at the rear I believe, used by technicians or things like that. I saw this dear man's body quiver with the impact. Then fall. I was at his side in an instant and the light of life was still in his eyes. But it was growing dimmer. I bent over him and seized his hand and could barely feel the feeble grasp that he returned.

"My friend . . ." he said, then coughed and his lips turned carmine with his very life's blood. "My dear friend . . . I am going now. It is up to you . . . to carry on . . . our work. Be strong. Promise me . . . that you will build the world we both wanted . . ."

"I promise, I promise," I said, my voice hoarse with emotion. His saintly eyes were closed, but he must have heard me for his dying hand gave one last tremor as it tightened on mine. An instant later it went limp.

Then his loyal wife was pushing me aside, seizing him up with a strength I did not know she possessed, then others rushed to her aid.

"It cannot be!" she cried, and my heart went out to her in her moment of pain. "It cannot be—he cannot be dead—doctors, ambulance! He must be saved!"

They hurried him off and I did not stop them. She would know soon enough. I dropped into my seat and looked down in despair, then saw for the first time his noble blood upon my hand. Reverently I took my handkerchief from my breast pocket and pressed it to the red droplets, soaking them up, then carefully refolding the linen to preserve them forever.

And that I have done. The handkerchief is before me now, under a glass dome filled with a neutral gas that will preserve its fabric intact for eternity. It stands beside the case holding the crown jewels, discovered in Zapilote's private chamber where that creature used to fondle them for some perverse reason.

You all know the rest. Thousands of you were at his funeral. Nor is he forgotten. His simple grave is still visited by multitudes every day.

You know about his enemies as well, for that story has been writ most often. How the crowd surged to their feet and cried "Death to the Despot" and were about to throw themselves upon that monster Zapilote and tear the flesh from his body with their fingers. How he quailed before their wrath and how he looked upon death and was possessed by fear.

It was then, at that very moment, that Harapo's noble wife returned and stood before the quailing creature and raised her hand and the crowd was silent and she did address them.

"Hear me, oh people of Paraiso-Aqui, hear me. My dear husband is dead. It is over. But do not throw away the world that he died to give you. Abide by the rule of law, even when dealing with pieces of filth like the wicked Zapilote. Condemn him for his crimes but do not kill him. My husband did not believe in murder—so do not commit it in his name. I thank you."

I am not so proud that I would deny that there were tears in my eyes when she spoke. There was not a dry eye in that immense hall. For even Zapilote was weeping with relief.

His widow left Paraiso-Aqui the very next day, for his memory was everywhere here. I saw her walk into the spaceship, turn and wave once, then go on. Behind her were the two brave young men, James and Bolivar. She left all of her possessions behind. There were just the few bags that the steward carried into the ship behind her. The spacelock swung shut and I have never seen her since.

The rest is history. Though I had no wish to serve in the high office of President I could not refuse that good man's dying wish. I have labored for you to the best of my abilities, and the majority have declared that I have served you well. I am satisfied. The scoundrels who terrified this world are no longer with us. They were condemned at public trial and found guilty. Our appeal to the Interstellar League of Justice was answered and you all know how they were removed to the prison planet of Calabozo. Every corrupt judge and policeman went. Every last one of the Ultimados who terrified this planet for two centuries. All gone. We have been purified. And they are all alive and, if not well, at least surviving. For it is a matter of record that there are no warders on Calabozo, just a few robots. The planet is wild and has a severe climate. All of the prisoners there must grow their own food and fend for themselves for the rest of their natural lives. They are their own destinies. They cannot escape. It is a well-deserved fate for that scurrilous crew.

My story must end at this point. As your president it was a far, far better thing that I did than I have ever done; it is a far, far better world we have here than we have ever known. We have Him to thank for that. He will live in our memories forever. Thank you, dear friend, and good-bye.

Still Another Afterword

As the saying goes, it's hard to really kill a stainless steel rat. But it's easy enough to tire one out. I don't know what souvenirs Angelina had put into the suitcases, bars of gold perhaps, but they were slowly tearing my arms out at the sockets. I staggered up the ramp behind her and the boys and on into the security of the spaceship. It wasn't until the airlock closed behind us that I felt free to drop them and straighten up.

"James," I said, "or Bolivar. Would either of you like to help your aging father by carrying these bags the rest of the way?"

I pressed my fist against my aching back and my spine crackled nicely. What a relief. Then I saw two passengers turning my way and I grabbed up the bags again just as Bolivar was reaching for them.

"No young sir, not your job to carry bags, not on this ship. Old Jim will carry them. This way madam, kind young gentlemen, I'll show you to your suite of cabins." I tottered off with my family following close behind. Only when the cabin door had closed behind me did I drop the awful bags and groan with relief.

"You poor dear," Angelina said, patting my hand then leading me to the chair. "Now just sit there for a bit while I see if I can find something that might cheer you up."

I peeled off the gray moustache and eyebrows and hurled the gray wig from me while she bent to open the suitcase. The lid flipped back to reveal row after row of dark bottles nestled into a soft protective bed. Angelina took one out and held its dusty form up to the light.

"Hundred-year-old ron. Lots of it. A little souvenir of Paraiso-Aqui that I thought you might enjoy. Let me pour you a drop to see if it was bruised in travel."

"Light of my life!" I gushed with sincere admiration. "You

182

are too kind." It was pure paradise as it trickled down my throat. She smiled and nodded approval.

"It was the least I could do for you after you had been assassinated."

"It did go well, didn't it? That was a good shot, James. Hit right square in the center of the bag of blood which squirted nicely. Though I wish you had used a cartridge with a smaller charge. It hit the armor plating with enough force to knock me over backwards."

"Sorry about that. But I measured the distance, two hundred and nine meters. I needed a flat trajectory to hit precisely at that distance. Your medals made a neat target."

"It ended well, that's what counts." I sipped and smacked. "You had no trouble getting away?" This was the first time we had been able to talk since I had been killed.

"It went smoothly. Bolivar was running up the stairs an instant after the shot was fired. I left the gun where it was and joined him. Then we led the pack in a chase after the killer. It was never a problem. Even better, your friend, Colonel Oliveira, joined in the chase. We managed to side-track him into an empty alley."

"The dear colonel!" I cried. "You gave him my best regards?"

"We did. The robots on the prison planet have been pro-grammed to take his casts off in about a month."

"Better and better. I watched the news when I was passing as a tourist at the beach hotel. Everything seemed to go quite smoothly. Even the funeral. Very realistic. You would almost think that there was a real body buried in my grave."

"There is," Angelina said, suddenly very serious. "We have some good news and some bad news. The bad news is that one of our party workers named Adolfo was killed. He was our best operative in Primoroso, a card shark who helped rig a number of ballot boxes. He was shot by the Ultimados. They brought him to the hospital while you were there. He died a few minutes later. They couldn't find his friends, so we made the most of the opportunity."

"Poor Adolfo. He really wasn't a very good card player. May he rest in peace." I sighed and drank a silent toast to his memory. "And the good news?"

The twins looked glum as she told me. "Jorge and Flavia have been married. They were engaged for years but swore not to wed until their homeworld was free."

"How romantic. Sorry boys. But there are other girls in the galaxy. Now please tell me, what about the real Sir Hector?"

"We followed your instructions," Bolivar said. "Pumped him full of Zapilote's expensive geriatric drugs, shaved off his beard and gave him a face lift. He looks thirty years younger and can easily pass for his own son. Right now he is back at work on his research—taking up his 'father's' work where the old man left off. He still is not quite sure what happened to him, but the faithful family retainers are taking care of him."

"Well, if I must say so myself, that was a very neat operation. All of the ends tied up, the bad guys knocked out, the good marquéz running the whole show, peace and prosperity now the rule on Paraiso-Aqui. A little episode in the battle against injustice and boredom that we all can be proud of."

"I'll drink to that," Angelina said, popping the cork from a bottle. "One last glass of champagne before we all go on the wagon."

"It will hold down the ron," I said, accepting with thanks.

We raised our glasses on high and drained them. It was a joy to be alive in this pleasant universe, particularly with a family like mine. Then the champagne hit the aged ron and I felt a mild rumble in my midriff that was followed instantly by a quick blast of gastric fire. Angelina was right, it was time to go on the wagon.

After this bottle was finished, of course.

The Final Afterword—from the Author

A number of readers, from a number of countries, have written to me asking if there really is such a language as Esperanto. Jim diGriz speaks it like a native—as do most of the people he meets while involved in his illegal trade. Esperanto is doing fine in the future—but does it exist in the present?

It certainly does. It is a growing, living language with millions of speakers right around the world. It is easy to learn—and fun to use. There are many books, magazines and even newspapers published in Esperanto.

If you are interested in more information, The Stainless Steel Rat's advice—and mine as well—is to write a postcard to the following address:

ESPERANTO
P.O. Box 1129
El Cerrito CA 94530

It will change your life!

Harry Harrison

ABOUT THE AUTHOR

HARRY HARRISON is one of the most successful and respected authors of speculative fiction writing today. In a
career that spans over three decades, Harry Harrison has
written such novels as *Deathworld, To the Stars, Skyfall,
Make Room! Make Room!* and bestsellers such as *West
of Eden, Winter in Eden,* and the Stainless Steel Rat
series. Harrison worked as a commercial artist, art direc-
tor and editor before turning to writing full time. A past
president of the World Science Fiction Association, he is
also a noted anthologist, editing the acclaimed Nova
series and co-editing the highly praised *Decade* and
Year's Best SF volumes with British author Brian Aldiss.
Harry Harrison was born in Stamford, Connecticut, has
made his home in Mexico and in several European countries over the years, and now lives in Ireland. His newest
novel, *Return to Eden,* will be published by Bantam
Spectra in July, 1988.

The Works of Harry Harrison

☐ **To The Stars** (26453-2 * $4.95/$5.95 in Canada) This omnibus edition includes the complete text of the novels in this blockbuster trilogy: **Homeworld, Wheelworld** and **Starworld.** Jan Kulozik, a brilliant young electronics engineer on 23rd-century Earth, risks his life to free the world's oppressed millions, to sever Earth's tyrannical rule over its far-flung star colonies and to restore humanity's heritage.

☐ **West of Eden** (26551-2 * $4.50/$4.95 in Canada) In a world where dinosaurs still exist, the young human Kerrick grows to manhood in the midst of the Yilane—cold blooded, intelligent reptiles—and uses his knowledge of their ways to become the humans' leader, and the dinosaurs' most feared enemy.

☐ **Winter In Eden** (26628-4 * $4.50/$4.95 in Canada) In this sequel to **West of Eden,** Kerrick must embark on a quest to rally a final defense against the Yilane, who have discovered that a new ice age is coming and are attempting to reconquer human territory.

☐ **Return to Eden** (05315-9 * $18.95 in hardcover/ $23.95 in Canada) The saga begun in **West of Eden** and **Winter in Eden** reaches its stunning conclusion. Kerrick leads his people to a safe haven only to discover that without effective weapons they are terribly vulnerable, and that his Yilane enemy Vainte, outcast from her people, stalks him, seeking his death.

Buy these books now on sale wherever Bantam Spectra books are sold, or use this page to order:
